TIGHT CINCHES
AND SHORT GRASS

TIGHT CINCHES
AND SHORT GRASS

FORWARD WRITTEN IN MEMORY OF RUSSELL CLINT GOODWIN

RUSSELL CLINT GOODWIN

TATE PUBLISHING
AND ENTERPRISES, LLC

Published by Tate Publishing & Enterprises, LLC
127 E. Trade Center Terrace | Mustang, Oklahoma 73064 USA
1.888.361.9473 | www.tatepublishing.com

Tate Publishing is committed to excellence in the publishing industry. The company reflects the philosophy established by the founders, based on Psalm 68:11,
"The Lord gave the word and great was the company of those who published it."

Published in the United States of America

ISBN: 978-1-68270-801-9
Fiction / Westerns
16.02.03

To my guardians, Clint and Emma Goodwin.

CONTENTS

FOREWORD

Russell's children loved him dearly. He is survived by Jody Bammann, Linda Stone, and Clint Goodwin. His oldest son, Mike Goodwin, passed to heaven in 1988. The surviving children offered the following thoughts:

> He used to call me Jody Blonde, hence the nickname, which I adopted many years ago. My earliest memory of time spent with Dad is when we actually "cut" a record together at a local recording studio.
>
> At age 2, my contribution was probably a few gurgles and giggles while he did most of the singing and strumming. However, I understand he did coax me to belt out a few words to "You Are My Sunshine." From there, a major influence on me was an interest and appreciation of music and fine arts of all genres. I frequently enjoyed watching him paint, carve out figures from blocks of redwood, and make music on a variety of stringed instruments. He was a very talented man.

As of then and now, my sincerest hope is that his talents will continue on through his present and future generations. He would be proud of how that hope is being realized.

—Jody Bammann, daughter

It is really cool to have had a dad as unique and interesting as Russell Goodwin, and each of us kids inherited at least one of his talents or interests. I'm really proud that he passed down his horsemanship abilities to me because the ten years that I rode as a professional jockey were so much fun and gave me so many good memories. Thanks, Dad!

—Linda Stone, daughter

My father and grandfather—Poppy—sat outside together, many times, on our picnic table playing dominoes and drinking Schlitz beer during the summer months. The Texas-size mosquitoes never bothered them during their games, since Dad screened in the front porch. Dad would say, "Come here, Mark. How is my son?" I always scrunched when his unshaven face pressed against mine. Dad would show his affection by pinching my ears.

The two war-torn veterans permitted me to watch them play dominos. During those family moments, my two war heroes talked about their service to our nation. My father and grandfather did not have one positive thing to say about the enemies they fought. Dad mumbled imprecations. Poppy would puff his pipe a couple of times and mumble, "The damn krauts killed my friends," then blow a smoke circle into the air. I knew not what their hearts were feeling, until years later when I carried a weapon myself into the fields of battle. Now I understand.

Dad said he was a "duration sailor." Honorably discharged in 1945, he returned to Texas ranching. He did not have an easy go of it. The sounds of war echoed in his mind every day thereafter. He found peace in his art and creativity from the bottle. Unfortunately, the latter killed him. War memories haunted him—memories only known to him and his shipmates who endured horrific naval battles in the Pacific Theater. He talked little about the war. He despised the enemy. I could not understand his dismay. Those reasons died with him in 2002.

—Clint Goodwin, son

THE NEPHEW

Late one night at a place called the Muleshoe Ranch, the drovers had gathered in the bunkhouse. They were there for two reasons, both of which involved the nephew. One was a darn good reason, they figured: a poker game, but the second reason was even better.

Mr. Henry Black was quite a big cowman; his cattle numbered in the thousands, and he employed plenty of drovers. Mr. Black's nephew had drifted down from Kansas City that summer to visit for a spell. He was one of them there city slickers, so it's been told. And all the drovers knew it. And my granddad, a drover, knew it. More than likely, Mr. Black knew it. The drovers said the nephew was always pestering and frolicking, mostly getting in the way of operations. So that night, the drovers invited the nephew to join in their friendly, little, old ranch poker game, so to speak.

Coal light flickered on crow's feet faces. The enthusiasm ran high, and the drovers crowded around the table. The bets were on, the stakes were high, and the nephew was right in among them, right where the drovers wanted him. Had he wanted to leave, he would have no easy escape.

It happened like the drovers figured. Before the cards were dealt all the way around the table, somebody called somebody a double-beaming snake belly or a dirty, double-blaming card thief. That second somebody's chair legs grated across the floor and out from under the table. The table might just have been turned over. As that second somebody stood up, he pulled out a great big pistol. The first somebody was doing the same.

The startled nephew began backing up, but he didn't have much place to go, except maybe up. The click of gun hammers falling in place must have been pretty loud to someone standing so close to the operators. The nephew's feet began moving but he wasn't. The drovers then began to take sides, and the nephew's fears took off like a scared horse. He just knew there were a hundred guns in plain view and he was in the middle!

Actually, fifteen guns went off at the same time the lights went out. After the first volley died down, the sound of a bunch of running feet sounded through the darkness—only it was one set. The nephew ran over a table, through a chair, over a bedroll then out the door that opened to the stairs outside, only it took a little time for him to figure out which way the darn thing opened.

Outside, another story was waiting. Of all things, somebody had stretched a ketch rope about knee-high between the porch's gallery posts. In the darkness, those fast-moving legs became tangled in the rope. In fact, they became tangled with it twice. The rope won. On the hot trail to the main house, the nephew yelled out in the darkness, "Oh, Uncle Henry, come quick! They are killing one another, and they tried to break both my legs!"

MR. EWELL DAVIS'S TRADIN' AND MERCANTILE STORE

On the Clearfork River, there was a store near a wagon crossing. The building was shotgun long, narrow and high. The owner was the same width and height, and weighed about three hundred pounds. The time and the place also swayed in the direction of the building's owner. Mr. Davis had as much money as he had weight. You see, the 1870s had brought big things to big men, especially to Ewell Davis and his Tradin' and Mercantile Store on the Clearfork River. If one thing didn't bring in money, he would find something that would.

A lot of land had been acquired up and down the river. About that time, the Katy railroad had pushed through, and lo and behold, it stopped just short of the Tradin' and Mercantile Store, maybe a hundred yards or so. About this time, the buffalo hunters started hauling in hides from out west. Davis's Tradin' and Mercantile started paying one dollar to two dollars per hide. At one time thousands of hides were stacked behind his store. When the numbers increased to a couple of carloads, Davis shipped them to Kansas City. There the hides netted him nine dollars to ten dollars a piece.

The buffalo hides vanished with the buffalo, and trail herds of longhorn cattle took their place, for drovers had a good crossing on the Clearfork River. That was when Davis's expansion of horses and cattle began. But most of the drovers decided to trail drive on north because the prices were better than those Davis offered here on the Clearfork.

Mr. Davis had purchased a yellow wheel buggy to survey his large holdings. Now these buggies were not designed for a three hundred-pound passenger. The buggy step, however, which was attached to the buggy frame, went by the wayside under Mr. Davis's bulk. So he had a blacksmith forge what you could call an iron ladder. This was placed where the buggy step used to be. On one of his excursions around the country, one of his neighbors attended this drive. The two saw a small black boy pitching hay from a horse-drawn wagon. The neighbor commented on how much work that young boy could turn out. Davis commented in return, "Wish I had his appetite."

Even in the ablest condition, a fat man was supposed to be jolly-minded and make-and-take practical jokes. But when someone else jokes, dealing with the jokes often sours a jolly, fat man.

The weather around the river country had been unsettled for the past few months. It was early spring, and rain clouds hung like wet sponges on a clothesline. Lightning danced around from treetop to treetop and back again, and thunder had that earsplitting rip. It was late in the evening when three slickered horsemen made their way through the watery curtain. They pulled up on the lee side of the Tradin' and Mercantile Store. A dim light flowed through a flyspecked window glass. The riders noticed a great bulk hunched over a rolltop desk. They also noticed that each time a lightning bolt struck near the river and was followed by a gigantic thunderclap, the man at the desk rushed to the window and peered into the wet blackness, then went back to the desk. It was quite plain that the owner of the Tradin' and Mercantile Store wasn't quite sure about his safety or the strength of the walls of his trembling structure.

Well, the men in this outfit, who had been hunting cows all day, were very well acquainted with their greedy friend, Ewell Davis, and they decided that one more event for the day seemed to be in order.

One of the drovers noticed a 2 × 4 about four feet long propped against the side of Mr. Davis's building. He picked this up and rode to the end of the building. There, the rider waited on his horse for the right time.

In those days, buildings were set on blocks about two to three feet off the ground. The siding was what they called board and batten, a style which essentially had a washboard effect, I say "essentially" because in those days lumber used for building was not "cut to dimensions." Anyway, when a lightning bolt shied off a nearby pecan tree, the rider held the end of the 2 × 4 against the vertical siding, and after spurring his mount, he ran down the length of the Tradin' and Mercantile Store. It so happened that a thunderbolt jarred the board walls about the same time the end of the 2 × 4 met with a glass window. That was a big noise and a big scare for a big man!

That way Moss Ageat told it later, Mr. Davis was more than a might uneasy in that store: "When me and th' boys pulled up at the back door, the door burst open into th' white lightning flashes. Mr. Davis, at a full run, disengaged himself from that there building. We remember seein' that bulk go flyin' through the air. It were a mighty jump. From up in th' air a mighty voice warned us that the Tradin' and Mercantile store was headin' for the river!"

THE WASSON BROTHERS
OR MUSICAL WAGONS

In the tears that followed the years in the War Between the States, some kind of revival settled over the land of the Clearfork River country. One could have said it was a revelation—a revelation for miles around, a dinner on the ground at a place called Brush Arbor, the spoken word of the Lord, and as such. Sometimes, these camp meetings lasted and lasted, and sometimes these camp meetings got a little bit boring, especially to the younger set, many of whom complained, "There ain't nothing to do!"

Parents replied with, "Well, you'll just have to set and don't be wrestlin' in the dirt!"

"Well," the children countered, "where else do a feller wrestle? Besides, we're gonna get that big 'un…"

Now, Mr. and Mrs. Wasson were servants to the public and considered themselves servants of the Lord. Their four boys, as always, attended these camp meetings with them.

It seemed like the old, old story, Shall We Gather by the River? Sometimes, the river was many miles away for some participants, and they had to travel by wagon and team.

So the Wasson brothers were young, and the days were getting old. Finally, it was time to depart from the camp meeting. The Wasson boys made it a point to be among the wagons when the reverend officiated the last word about heaven above. All these wagons had already been packed and hitched, and other personal belongings placed within the sideboards. Like the other kids, the Wasson brothers had fallen asleep waiting for the long trip home. The Wasson parents returned to their wagon and pulled out the campground.

About this time, a wagon pulled out and then pulled back in, as did another and another, till the whole kit and caboodle ended up back at Brush Arbor. It sure was not for the Word of the Lord, but the word of the breadwinners.

"Where's my Willie?" "Where's my Myra?" parents questioned, then went searching for their own.

Well, the Wasson boys had changed kids with wagons or wagons with kids, whichever come first. As the Wasson parents put their young'uns in the correct wagons, all four remained asleep. On the way home, they didn't get that big un, either.

RAWHIDE DON'T MAKE LOVE CALLS

Emma Wasson was a fine young woman in the days of cattle drives and farming. Her father owned the Wasson General Mercantile Store. Mr. Wasson was also the area's practicing veterinarian. Clint was a young drover for Mr. Henry Black, who owned about fifty thousand cows that ranged over a lot of hills, rivers, and brush country. Mr. Black's ranch had a cow wagon with about a hundred head of saddle horses. Now, for those who don't know what a cow wagon is, it is the mobile home for drovers. There, a drover gathers grub; he even sleeps underneath the wagon bed when it rains.

Clint spent all his time gathering and driving cows in the spring and late fall. From late fall, he planned to spend all the time he could escorting Miss Emma Wasson, that is, if Miss Emma's father did not object. In those days, a fellow just didn't go out with a lady. A fellow first asked her elders if he could escort their daughter to a picnic, dance, or a church social. Attending the latter was mostly Miss Emma's choice, which, in turn, always had the approval of her elders.

Now in those days, a cow drover was like one of King Arthur's knights setting on a cow horse. That fellow behind that hickory shirt and wearing spurred boot heels never broke a girl's heart. A cow drover was the most trusted man in the land. His word was his bond. Most cattle thieves or outlaws sure never were in a social gathering in the drover's part of the cow country. So be it.

One fall afternoon, another fellow, not Clint, escorted Miss Emma to a church social and then took her to a picnic on the banks of the river.

But another source was conjuring up a pot of fortune at this time. Will Black, son of the cattle owner, had passed on this little tidbit of information about Emma and her escort's whereabouts to his friend, Clint. And this started wheels turning. The two went to the barn and pulled out what was known as a cat's head. Nearly all cow drovers kept things like this stashed away for such emergencies.

Two things make a cat's head: rawhide and a wooden keg. Horseshoes were shipped to the ranch in these kegs so you know they were well made. The keg top and bottom were knocked out, and wet rawhide was stretched across one end. The wooden staves were pulled tighter than the proverbial fiddle string. In turn, a half-inch hole was cut out in the center of the rawhide. A rawhide thong that was a bit thicker than this hole was then cut and forced through a half-inch hole. Next, wooden handles were put on the ends of the thong. After supplying a good coat of rosin to the thong, the contraption was ready for action. Pulling that thong back and forth through the hole gave the hair on the head a stand-up sensation. In fact, a good cat's head operator could get some different effects if he played the instrument just right.

Clint and Will, who were experts at playing the cat's head, made their way to the shaded and brushy bank of the river by the side of the church. They got real close. Clint could even smell the fried chicken Miss Emma had laid on the checkered cloth. Hell, it must have been one of Mrs. Wasson's!

Describing a noise or sound accurately without actually using the noise or sound itself takes a giant leap of the imagination, so bear with me. Now, that rawhide thong outfitted with wooden handles jerked through the rawhide keg end and a real ground-quivering howl set up which literally shook the bushes. It also shook up Miss Emma's escort. The cat's head went wailing again when Will pulled the thong in the opposite direction.

Both Will and Clint agreed this turned out to be a better performance than they had expected. The picnickers were startled asunder and swooned, especially the one wearing the striped britches. Mrs. Wasson's fried chicken was dropped on the checkered tablecloth from shaky hands that no longer knew what they were doing. With a sudden movement, Emma's escort skimmed posthaste over the ground toward the river. Later, all three—Will, Clint, and Emma—agreed that striped britches actually walked on water for about five feet, then motored to the other bank. The scenario was another rendition of Meet me on the Opposite Shore or Shall We Gather by the River?

Clint asked Miss Emma if she had gotten scared when the monster raised its evil head. "Oh, yes," was the answer, "until I heard you and Will laughing!"

THE GUNS OF THE MULESHOE HERD

Early in the spring, Mr. Henry Black wanted to start a trail herd, about three thousand head, up north. Right now, I need to clarify a statement. The old trail drovers of that day and time went up north but never stated going back down south.

On the way north, the river, Big Red, had a problem with crossing a herd of cattle. Of course, what I'm saying is that the Big Red was up, that is full of water running downhill to the Gulf of Mexico. Of course, it was never high enough to prevent crossing three thousand head of cattle.

When water runs off the brims of hats the way it runs off the tips of longhorns, you can trust that everything the drovers have will get a soaking, even the bedrolls. The drovers just ride along and eventually get dried out by the warm, spring sun only to get soaked again in about the same length of time. After thirty days of this, drovers sometimes lose their tempers.

About halfway on this trip north, Mr. Black decided to loose the herd in a green valley. When the cattle went to market, he wanted them to look good. And, of course, when cattle feel good in the springtime, they like to run. Their kind of running is mean running.

But now, the drovers had been resting up and drying out after the wet spell. It didn't take half the drovers to loose a herd of three thousand heads of cattle, but Clint was one of those who took on the job. He was unlucky enough though to get the brushy side of the valley, and, of course, there was a little creek and the little creek bottom to go with it. And, of course, some of the old three-year-old steers wanted in that bottom. Before Clint could ride to that spot, five head had beaten him into the brush. On seeing them go in, Clint decided to run the d——n hell out them to get them out there. Cattle like to hide in those brushy areas, and it can be d——n difficult to find them.

But let me tell you a little more about Clint. Clint was raised back in Arkansas by his uncle, who was the town marshal. Now, in that neck of the country, the marshal's homestead was part of the jail. Sometimes Clint's uncle had to produce a long-barreled colt to get his point across to objectors. As a small boy, Clint didn't like guns, not did it impress him that his uncle needed to use his gun to get others to plead uncle. Fifteen years later, Clint was making a living chasing cows over hill and dale, and sometimes in the Indian territory. Most of the drovers carried a sidearm or a booted rifle. Not Clint.

On this day, Clint had gotten those five d——n "bunch quitters" turned back, and he was pushing them at a pretty good clip out the creek bottom using both ends of the ketch rope. Engrossed in this business, horseman Clint didn't notice the other two horsemen. They also rode out the brush onto open ground. They were coming on at a little faster clip than Clint with his five steers. What finally captured Clint's undivided attention was the war whoop yells and the waving of what looked like shiny, long knives and perhaps a war axe or two.

Clint put the spurs to Dunny's sides and the ketch rope across his rump. Surprised by the added energy of his rider, Dunny went sailing past the five steers and on up the gentle slope. And the long knives, war clubs, and yelling were right behind. Seems Clint had an escort home.

Bill, the camp cook, was standing at the chuck box and saw what all was taking place down the slope. Later, he said old Dunny was packing all the meat, bones, and leather lighter than one of his pancakes. The two Indians were really no problem, but they looked a little gritty. And they were cutting thin slices out of thick air with their shiny weapons.

Heading for the cow wagon, where the cook was, Dunny was fast putting distance between Clint and those pesky Indians. Clint had conveyed to Dunny the extra danger that was running pell-mell, yelling and waving all those weapons.

Clint knew Charley kept a long-barreled colt in the chuck box, but he had a little time to search for it. When Bill came around the wagon, Clint asked where Charley's pistol was. That's when the buckskins arrived, and Bill told Clint that Charley had taken his gun with him. That's when Bill asked him if he had brought company home for dinner. This did not sit too well with the unmounted rider. Then the two Indians just set on their mounts and grinned from ear to ear. The Indian's long, braided black hair bobbed around, and their black eyes danced with laughter. Bill said later it was kind of hard for him not to do a little snickering himself.

Through Bill's knowledge of sign language, Texican talk, Indian lore, and a little cow savvy, Bill explained to Clint, "See that slender buck there?"

Of course, Clint could see that slender buck. That was the one with the long steel blade.

"Yeah, well, that's Fleet-Steel." The Indian grinned more on hearing his name spoken.

Just the same, no matter who he was, Clint was going to keep his eyes peeled on that one. That name fit the Indian to a tee. "That's a d——n good hoss he's on. He probably stole it somewhere," Clint replied.

"When I was a small walkey," Bill continued, "my father talked a heap to me about the heap big yellow horse, the heap big yellow horse that has hooves of the wind. I knew one day I would see one, and one day I would test one. And this day, I have tested. And this day it is true."

"And this day you might have weighed a little more with a little lead." Clint tossed back.

"My father is right. The heap big yellow horse has hooves of the prairie wind. Thank you for letting me test."

"Test, hell!" Clint stormed over to Dunny, loosened the horse's cinch, and walked him around a bit to cool him down, so to speak. What the heck, thank me! Clint thought. He remembered recently hearing about some buckskins ploshing off some general called Custer, something to do with a cavalry outfit. Thanks!

Months later at the railhead, Bill spotted Clint and Charley unsaddling their horses. Bill bellowed in his mind, What is that, some kind of metal strapped around Clint's middle? Oh, hell, he'll shoot himself in the foot!

THEN THERE WAS A GATHERIN'

I

Anyone who has never been on a cow gathering has never really missed anything except bad country, bad horses, bad weather, bad company, and bad pay.

Like all the rest of the cowmen, Mr. Black scheduled two roundups: one in the spring and one in the fall. The one in the fall was to let you know it is; the one in the spring was to state, "This is it." City slickers kind of always looked at the rained-on, stained horsemen who battled range, brush, and river as having—in modern terms, so to speak—elevators that don't go all the way up. But many of these "knothole" geniuses bought and used the fruits of the cow drovers' work. Oh, those city clickers with their soft suits, soft talk, and nice little cow hide—what do you call them? Attaché cases, that's it. Out rider of the purple sage who sets on a sunset hill is saddled with enough responsibility to make one of them there Yale-hail scholars ashamed of himself. Even a cow drover knows Yale makes locks. The drover who went into business had to show into that business, and it took a lot of showing.

By the way, cow drovers are not what city slickers call them. City slickers call them cowboys, oh, yeah, like in cowboy hats and cowboy boots, amen and amen. Sounds like one of those sunset Western songs by one of those vaporizing musicians, doesn't it?

It seems this underpaid critter, who wore a wide-brimmed hat and high-heeled boots, for thirty dollars a month or less, would straddle a one-hundred-dollar horse, get seven others to back him up, so to speak, and lope, not gallop, out onto the range and without a gaiter. Why, all these smart city slicker teachers can't even teach their smartest students how to write their own name! Talk about modern backwoods! Roy Rogers taught Trigger to write his name, and, by God, a horse is a dumb animal!

So this is here dumb butt, as many city slickers would say, enters a world where he is expected to care for and mother cows, calves, steers, heifers, bulls, studs, mares, colts, windmills, fences, wagon teams, harnesses, saddles, and barns, as well as tend to both humans and animals doctoring field cuts, illnesses, and the like. Then there's water holes, water gaps, dogs, cats, pigs, chickens, and rattlesnakes.

The ace card to ranching is water. Next in line are grass, hay, grain, cow feed, feed troughs, brands, operations, vaccines, and being kind to saddle horses, boss's wife, and particularly the cook and them sourdough biscuits. And amen to them biscuits. All them things are taken up around the homeplace, so to speak. There's a few more responsibilities I could list, like moving three thousand heads of cattle on a dimly lit trail. But, of course, the average city slicker can listen to some of that Western music— the songs that are set to noise—or get a real picture from Hollywood to help him figure out the rest of what it's like to work a ranch. Sometimes they even call that hullabaloo country. My, my. The roundup would soon start.

Back in the Muleshoe country, Mr. Black's cattle had roamed miles from ranch headquarters. But the Muleshoe Ranch first needed to round up some men. Sometimes different folks took up residence in these vast areas. The word "nester" came down the trail from Kansas. It seems that state was filling up that prairie land with plows and barbed wire, which would soon alter the way cattle would be delivered into that state. What was called a gathering or a roundup in those days was called a cow hunt by the real drovers. Nesters often helped in the roundup.

Word was out that Mr. Black wanted so-and-so to help deliver some cattle up the trail. In response to Mr. Black's request, two drovers rode up to the front of a nester's house. The drovers helloed the house, which is still a custom, but they got no answer, so they rode around back. One drover looked in an open window.

"Wall, it looks as effen they moved."

"I believe yer right. Th'lookin' glass and water pitcher's gone."

Those nesters must have flown the coop, so to speak.

So the drovers would have to look elsewhere.

II

It so happened that Moss Ageat was an expert at his trade which was cow hunting, and Muleshoe Ranch wanted him pretty regular. Mr. Black even asked Moss to bring his wife and move out to Muleshoe. Though he refused, for he had a little farm and stock of his own, he still helped the Muleshoe outfit push stock up the trail. Well, word was sent to Mr. Ageat that Mr. Black would sure like his help. Word came back that Mr. Ageat himself sure needed some help too. So Mr. Black sent all his drovers and a packhorse with grub down to Moss. Fourteen hands picked fifty acres of cotton. Mrs. Moss Ageat did some mighty fine cooking with that Mr. Black sent down. Good cooking always kept a cow drover—surely not cotton picking!

III

Sometimes gathering trail drovers could just be interesting as it was dangerous. Mr. Black ranged his cattle south of the Muleshoe Ranch in a section that contained cedar breaks, low hills—and a homesteader named Doesier, who was a gunman.

Since Charley was the oldest one on the ranch, Mr. Black sent him and Clint down south not only to check on the Muleshoe cattle but also to drop by Doesier's place and tell him that Mr. Black was getting ready to send a herd north. Thus, the old and the young were destined to parley with a gunman.

One the way, Charley tried to reason with young Clint, who at the moment, was not cherishing the thought of kicking a sore-tailed bear or agitating Colonel Colt—Doesier's nickname—who might be thinking they might be the law. But the way it was, Mr. Black wanted d——n good drovers, and Doesier was a d——n good drover. You see, this homesteader who, along with his wife, farmed a little strip of land some ten miles over had killed a fellow. The so-called "law" wanted to frame him as a murderer in what was really a case of self-defense. But Doesier had killed was a rich man's son, which complicated matters, as a lot of money always does. Doesier had made his break and ran from the law because he was not willing to stand in an already-made noose.

When the two Muleshoe riders rode up close to the plowed field, Charley started waving his "down-in-the-beam" hat. Clint spotted Doesier on the cultivator doing some plowing. Doesier waved back, then pulled up and stopped the plow alongside the two riders. Clint noticed a big Winchester rifle booted and hung on the plow's iron frame. There was also a dark-handled pistol tucked in his waistband. Clint sensed the open air of long, lost brothers as Doesier and Charlie greeted each other. Clint would later learn that these two men had known each other since their boyhood days. That was the real reason for Mr. Black sending Charley down to Doesier's in the first place. Of course Charley would go, and he would help his old friend out a bit. The plowing and planting was about over, but some firewood needed to be cut for the missus, and a couple of days' time would do it, then Doesier would help out Charley and Clint round up the cattle.

Clint rode off scratching his head. This trim, black-haired, mustached man who wears clothes that are washed and ironed, who keeps his hosses in top condition, and who provides for his wife and home, a killer gunman? Hell!

So it was that Doesier who joined the Muleshoe cow wagon on the cattle drive north. But this slim, trim man who set his saddle straight as a poker kept in a hidden action coiled inside his lithe body. And, of course, this always lets out a secret to a young cow drover. Clint made it an obsession to get to know this fellow, Doesier the gunman. He sure didn't carry his pistol like the rest. Clint noticed that every move Doesier made with horse or rope was instrumental. This was what Mr. Black called "top hand." No matter how long in the saddle, day or night, this man worked like a machine. A fellow just didn't go over to

Doesier's bed-ground and put his hands on him to wake him up, you better believe that. And if a conversation was going on, Doesier seemed to always be awake. Everybody knew or had that steel-trap feeling that Doesier's long-barreled colt was never far from his hand.

So it went. The cow drover Doesier stayed uncaptured for five years. There might have been some question that Doesier shot the man in self-defense, and there just might have been a little finagling going on down in the law department. Though Doesier was acquitted years later, at this time he was still a wanted man, and some of the drovers resented having to work with a man who had killed a fellow, regardless of the circumstances. So the drovers put a plan into action. They knew if they set up camp on the Red River, they would be close to a jailhouse. Thus, somebody in the outfit would make a try, that is, to capture Doesier the gunman.

Floyd was a big scrapping fellow. Just like all the other drovers, he spent many days in the branding pen wrestling down yearlings. About two months of this puts a thick shirt on a body. It seemed to Floyd that Doesier had developed a habit that any dumb drover could figure out. Doesier always waited till the others moved out of the way, like he did when they were catching horses, serving up grub, and even crawling into their sugans (bedrolls) at night. He was mighty careful.

At the end of a meal, the drovers would toss their tin hardware into the roundup pan, which sat on a chuck-box lid.

"Maybe at suppertime, when it is dark, maybe Floyd could kind of linger in the dark shadows on the off side of the wagon." One drover speculated on how to capture Doesier. "Maybe Floyd could just step out and grab Doesier from behind, you know, when he walks off from the roundup pan."

"Yeah," another drover added, "them other two drovers would be real close by when Floyd makes his move."

The men organized Doesier's capture and fully believed their plan would work, but Floyd began having second thoughts on the night he was to go through with capturing Doesier. He had more than two thoughts regarding the matter, that's for sure. He lived and slept with these thoughts. It sure was easy riding along thinking about the capture of a gunman. He wondered what the country paper would write. That black-handled colt, which tonight was gleaming in the lantern light and casting ghostly patterns on the sides of the blackened roundup pan, sure made him think.

Then Floyd heard the sound of clatter and his breathing increased. The problem was that his lungs weren't getting enough air at this particular location in the dark shadows. His mind was racing fast but his lungs couldn't keep up. Why, that little shrimp. He could be busted with one blow...But his movements are kinda swift...quick, yeah, kind of like lightning...yeah, quick. They say he is just quick with that black-handled colt. What the hell, there are lawmen around here...and maybe they don't want to find out how fast he is.

Floyd watched the trim figure dissolve into the night shadows. Doesier was heading for his sugans, which he had pulled away to one side. Doesier was going on guard at midnight. He's a good drover and a good man, thought Floyd. Leastways he believes in himself.

CHRISTMAS TREE CROSSING

The Muleshoe men were on the move again. Three thousand head of steers were strung out over low hills and dales. The drovers' duties depended on where they were placed in the herds. The swingers and flankers kept the herd together. The pointers at the front of the herd pointed the cattle in a given direction. By the way, the front of the herd is not much of a place to be if the herd gets "boggered" and starts running—it's called a stampede. The drags at the back keep the herd moving. The downside of the drags' job is that they get to enjoy a dense cloud of smelly dust and heavy dirt that follows them around no matter which way the wind is blowing. Off to the side rolls the chuck wagon and hoodlum wagon. This latter one carries branding irons, firewood, mule feed, a few choice items, and the hoodlum, the young man who obeys the bark of a cantankerous cook. The hoodlum's got his eyes set on a drover's job one day. Anything would beat his job. Anyway, behind the wagons, the wrangler grazes about a hundred heads of saddle horses. This group is called a remuda.

Soon, the cook and horse wrangler would pass the herd and make camp several miles ahead. Crossing the Clearfork River was not a big problem. The rail herd and outfit could just skip right by. The high riverbanks would break off to where there was nothing but low banks that led off onto a gravel bar. Sometimes there wouldn't even be a drop of water. But at this crossing, the water had risen to wheel hub deep on the wagons and was edging up the low-sloping banks. This was also a commercial crossing—in other words, a public highway. The dirt and rocks rose forty feet on each side. There, the water might be the same depth.

On the opposite side, the cook made his camp. Great pecan trees graced the rims of a large, verdant meadow. This would be where the wrangler would turn loose his remuda so they could graze on the tall grass. Farther on, the bottom land opened out onto a prairie. This was where the wagon boss would put the bed-ground.

Fifteen men can put away a lot of grub while out on the trail for several months, so the chuck wagon is the queen of hearts of any outfit. It follows that the cook is king—he's the one who's really in command of the outfit. The cook on this particular drive was a real jewel. He made delicious apricot pies and raisin pudding along with the daily menu, which included sourdough biscuits. This dough is made in the ranch kitchen a few weeks in advance, and it has to be fixed a certain way. After the fix, the dough is stored away in little wooden barrels.

An occurrence that happened late one night or early the following morning would change the crossing on the Clearfork River and maybe test the mentality of a darn good cook.

The last guard came into camp. A guard stays with the herd for four hours. The one who worked from twelve till four in the morning was supposed to wake the cook. But one night, he woke the cook and turned in to his sugans; some drovers opened one of those wooden barrels of sourdough. One of them was already open so there was plenty of sourdough—not for eating but for decorating. Let me give you a hint: even if it's June, think about Christmas.

The usual time for grub call was generally "dark thirty." The thinking was to get all the minor tasks over with early, then at first light, all attention could be put to use out there, on that there trail herd of cows, bulls, steers, and heifers— not necessarily in that order.

Well, at first light, the little tree glowed contentedly. The rising sun caught the dazzling decorations in all their glory. It was quite a different tree and stood out among all the other trees in the rest of the woodland.

The tree wasn't very tall, maybe arm's-length high. Nobody in his right mind would select this tree for such attention. One drover pointed this out to the cookie, as the cook was sometimes called. The low rays of the sun caught and coated every branch. The white strips off sourdough, just like tinsel, caught everyone's eyes, including the cook's. The drover's prank could have upset the cook. But instead the cook was amazed. The long strips of sourdough were starving to gain recognition, hanging there among the branches in the little tree. Those doughly ornaments sure did sparkle in the morning sun. Thus, the name Christmas Tree Crossing remained all during the trail-herd days. The name has stuck—even to this day.

THE INSPECTOR

One year Mr. Black had a lot of two-year-old heifers. He wanted to keep them for replacement cows. So a pasturing arrangement was made with Chief Fleetwood, who had control of a lot of land in the Indian nation. So with a trail herd going north, the replacement herd would be dropped in and dropped out when Mr. Black's men drove the herd through the Indian nation. Mothering three thousand homesick heifer yearlings north was always a difficult task. The yearling's line of thinking was, Look here, I'm a little wild, dumb brute, and you gotta figger out what I'm gonna do. That there goes fer you drovers and range hosses! As the inevitable happened, things fell into place.

One evening, on a riverbank, the day was fast fading away. The wagon boss had the herd on the bed-ground. And the drovers were studying the crossing for the herd the next day. Well, a lone rider came splashing across. They right then learned just where the shallow water was. Mr.

Black complimented the rider for he had all figured that section was the deepest spot in the river, not the shallowest.

Well, apparently a complete stranger can spot the owner of a trail herd. Maybe it's the way owners part their hair or trim their mustaches. The stranger rode alongside Mr. Black. He was a stranger, but not for long. For introductions, he stated he was a cattle inspector for the great state of Kansas. He has a pretty wife and two towheads. This old-time cowman who had once ramrodded the old-time Muleshoe Ranch took an old-time look at his old-time wagon boss, old-time Charley. But Charley and some old-time drovers had an old-time idea.

That night, the whole outfit, including the cook, got the word to move out, and by the sign of first light, that outfit had crossed the river where the stranger had and had moved a great number of miles north. There, the boss had the cook unpack the wagon and whip up some well-deserved grub. Later on, Clint related the quick movement of men, wagons, horses, and cows. You might say they flew the coop.

The stranger had ridden alongside the boss and had told his life history; that was a bad thing, especially down in Texas. His being a cow inspector from Kansas sure was a drawback, especially for the herd. Though he didn't know it, the inspector had just signed his death warrant. Any fool would know a Kansas cow inspector would condemn a Texas herd and the whole outfit would be forced to turn tail. The drovers all knew it, that's for sure.

So that night when the midnight guard came in to sugans, the drovers had other ideas besides sleeping, and they put one good idea into action. What they did was simply tied up this inspector, sugans and all, left him under a shade tree, and moved out. He would be seen easily from the road, though, so another trail outfit would come along and find him. He just might be a little more congenial toward them.

Out on the point, Mr. Black and Clint rode. With a whiskered grin spread across his face, Mr. Black turned to the young drover and said, "A word to the wise, any darn fool knows better than saying who he is around these parts."

TURKEY

The drovers then moved the herd across some dry country. The rattle of a dry gourd could be heard for half a mile. Cowmen can reason with a dry thought for want of water. A thirsty herd, on the other hand, which acts like locoweed powder has been blown up their noses, means trouble long before the zenith, especially to the saddle horses. When water-starved cows smell water, which may be miles away, they head in that direction. They don't just walk there, they run there. They figure if they don't get there quick, it'll all be gone.

Mr. Black had sent Charley and Clint out to search for this commodity. A length of time and distance brought the two riders in spotting distance of a column of blue smoke feathering its way into the blue haze. Smoke seen above means life down below. Charley figured it was a squatter about two miles away. They rode into the squatter's yard. Charley kept his hand close to his colt, and Clint stayed behind Charley. Some squatters don't like cows. But Charley and Clint smelled like cows, and where you find drovers, there's bound to be cows someplace, range cows that is. This is about the same feeling cowmen have with sheepmen, only worse.

Charley and Clint "helloed" the house. A tall, slim, hawk-faced form darkened the doorway. Charley asked the elder if he has any drinking water. A younger critter joined the elder to find out what was going on. Any kind of strange talking around these parts was intriguing.

This young critter standing beside the elder caught Clint's eye. Clint thought, My God, he looks just like a turkey.

Then the elder gave the boy a gentle shove in the direction of the nearby well. "Go fetch these har fellers some drinking water, Turkey!"

Before leaving, Turkey pointed out the way to the water. Three thousand head of cows would never know Turkey.

THE COOK AND THE MULES

Little occurrences happen on trail drives, that make life interesting, for instance, the wagon cook. It seems this character was always volatile. Turning stampedes in the blackest night sometimes is easier than making friends with a real riled-up cook. But a cook has the right to be a little sensitive when he has to put up with the drovers' ideas of comic relief, like hanging sourdough in tree branches or outing a fog in a dutch oven, which the unknowing cook puts on the fire. Moreover, in addition to cooking for a large number of hungry men, the cook had the added responsibility of assuming the role of doctor since he is always in the camp.

Anyway, in this particular situation, the problem for the cook wasn't man but animal. It seems the wagon team had a mind of its own. This mule team didn't mind the cook taking them up hills, and through and across flooded rivers and dry spells, they just didn't hanker the cook hitching them to the wagon.

After making camp in the evening, the horse wrangler took care of unhitching the mules, then turned them over to the night hawks. This lone man took care of the remuda throughout the night no matter what. In the morning, the night hawk brought them in and out them in a rope corral. Then he caught the mules and hitched them to the wagon. But drovers, like cows and horses, can get sick, and the night hawk became ill, so he was out to bed. The hitching job thus fell to the cook, who, along with the hoodlum, are the last to break camp. The hoodlum was to help the cook load, unload, and hitch up the wagons—well, maybe everything but the hitching.

The mules allowed the two men to do everything that needed to be done with putting on the harness and wagon tongue, but when it came to the inside tugs and that inside single tree hook, no siree! There was a double wrought-iron shoe nailed on a little white hoof, and it was on the end of a cocked hind leg, and all this was about two feet from the cook's noggin. Outside tugs, okay, inside tugs, no. But the cook wanted to go on wearing his hat naturally, so he took up all the links on the tug and drove off. This wasn't the best, but he figured it would work all right until he caught up with the horse wrangler. The operation was hooking a single tug onto a single tree hook. The cook had wasted traveling time trying to pacify these gall-darn blockheaded mules doing that…

Well, the next day was a day that went down into infamy. The Muleshoe outfit was bedecked with the arrival of Chief Fleetwood, the chief whom Mr. Black had a pasturing arrangement. His presents, five wives, and fifteen children drove up in an army horse-drawn ambulance. To the right and to the left fanned out some fifty odd buckskins. The same with the horses. Everything was bright and shiny.

Clint was saddling his horse when the brevet rode up in the little green valley. The brevet's horse was between Clint and his horse and his Indian outfit, and Clint was gonna keep it that away. Behind him was the river and open country. This Indian outfit made him uneasy because it reminded him of a raiding party. He remembered them squaws could butcher a steer and not even lose the beller. Mr. Black sure does some of the damnedest things, Clint thought, inviting Indians here. He had mighty fresh recollections of his recent experience with Indians.

Well, it wasn't massacre time. Mr. Black greeting the fabulous Indian leader. At a given signal, the welcome committee, those pesky Indians, swarmed into camp. The Indians knew a white man shook hands, but they wanted to do a better job—they wrung them! Heap big medicine! Outside of wringing arms, they simply poked around everywhere, including in the cook's chuck box and in the bed wagon; they even inspected the harnesses—all six sets—inch by inch. In fact, you could say they made themselves at home. Then Mr. Chief Fleetwood wanted to reciprocate and asked the Muleshoe Cattle Company to make themselves at home in his home. The chief even sent runners back to his village to spread the word: "The great white cow people will soon be arriving for a heap big celebration. I have spoken."

So the cattle were left in the little green valley. Seventy sets of hobbles were set on seventy saddle horses. If they wandered off, it would be toward Texas.

Now, the celebration the chief had in mind might be a trifle different from a cow wagon cook-off or a banquet down around the Texas Hotel in Fort Worth, Texas. In this particular village, the chief had built a wooden building with tepees all around it. This building, a big one-room affair, had a flat roof and opening for windows and doors on all sides, but the windows and doors weren't there, just the openings. A handmade table stretched from one end to the other with backless benches to set on. A big-armed chair was at the head of the table. Chief Fleetwood took dominion over this place and was the first to claim this chair. This was where nobility dwelled. The chief had been around and watched important folks act. But the chief wanted to hold his own shenanigans. So the chief, his wives, papooses, and buckskins lined up on one side of the long, hand-hewed table, and Mr. Black, the wagon boss, drovers, the cook, the hoodlum, and the horse wrangler lined up on the opposite side. All were a grinning. They all watched the chief, and they all did what the chief did. He sat down. They sat down. He grinned. They grinned.

Clint was about halfway down the table. What caught his eye was a long-barreled colt 44–40, a heavy duty, big bullet pistol lying alongside the chief's tin plate. If he raises that hog leg… Clint thought.

The heavyset squaws then set the table for the celebration and placed the banquet goodies on it. The first delivery was a young yearling, which more than likely had worn the Muleshoe brand. The whole thing was laid on the table in front of the chief. Clay pots were also placed here and there. The Indian corn pone had a fine aroma to Clint's nose. Throughout all this, the chief was still all smiles. This just didn't cotton to Clint because when someone played a trick on him, it seemed to always come with a smile.

Well, the chief did raise his hog leg gun. At the first shot, the whole Muleshoe outfit quit the whole Indian outfit. Those door and window openings proved a quick exit for cow drovers.

They just weren't quick on the draw, but moving on two legs was something else! Those door and window openings made for a hasty retreat. But the shooting didn't quit. Well, since the bullets didn't follow, the trail crew through the walls, the drovers sneaked a peek back inside. They noticed Mr. Black had taken up residence behind the smoking gunman. All the wives and papooses and buckskins were still a grinning and holding out their tin plates. Well, no

Indian would be worth his salt if he or she couldn't put a hand on the handle of a long-bladed knife. Yeah, some of them carried two about their bodies.

But this was a heap big celebration, and Chief Fleetwood wanted not only to cut up that beef but also do it in an artistic way! Original, they call it. The chief's way. With a four-prong fork and a smoking 44–40, the chief shot big chunks off that roasted yearling to the delight of his fifteen wives, papooses, and the buckskins—and to the Muleshoe outfit if they would come back inside! But you know the line about wild horses…

Back in the cow camp, thoughts ran through heads like rocks rolling down a hillside. There would be no more celebrations till this first celebration was complete, and it never would be! That quart bottle would simply keep its lid screwed on, and they'd hide the bottle better.

FIREWATER AND FIREWOOD

The Indian village, which was a gathering place, had a few houses and a lot of tepees. It was kind of like a trading place. Let me tell you about one of its characters.

When the buckskins spied white eyes riding around the range, they would seek out their presence, especially if the Indians knew there was firewater around someplace.

A young drover just happened to notice a drunk Indian at Chief Fleetwood's celebration. It seemed one such buckskin had beaten the rest to a favorite watering hole. Being in this so-called "state," the buckskin rode over to his tepee leading another horse. He jumped down and staggered into what he figured was his tepee and left the two horses ground hitched. But with even greater speed than he had gone through the flap opening, he picked up someone on the way out. In even shorter time, the drunken buckskin learned this surely was not his tepee—or his squaw! She leveled what seemed to be a piece of firewood on the buckskin. This time he made straight, not crooked, tracks.

His ground-hitched horses seen him heading their way. They figured they were in the way and had nothing else to do but tuck tail out there. They heard some kind of squaw talk that kept getting louder and louder and then the grunts of the sodden buckskin.

Well, the saddle horse went one way, and the horse with the long rope went another—that is, on each side of the tepee. The drover noticed about four tepees went down in this taut rope action. And there was plenty of action. There were four more big squaws with four more big sticks of firewood. The inebriated buckskin became a sober foot-running buck.

DOC BALL

Doctor Ball was an outstanding man. He was not only a doctor but also a good man inside who filled out his clothes. He was honest, upright, and a blessing to the little community. His word was bond. In those days, there on the banks of the Clearfork River, money was commodity that wasn't spread around too thick. Sometimes Doc Ball would take chickens, pigs, or a sack of feed as payment for doctoring a patient. Once at a church gathering on the Lord's Day, when the collection was being taken up, Doc Ball dropped his pocket watch into the collection plate. He told the elder that he and his wife were saving to build themselves a house.

One time, a real complicated case drove up in Doc Ball's front yard. The front room of his house was his office and clinic. It was the biggest room in the house. Glancing out the window, Doc Ball recognized his old friend, another doctor from down south, approaching in a hack. But the way his friend was setting in the hack was a little unusual. He was holding a handful of hair and looking straight ahead. Doc Ball soon realized his friend was holding up his own head! Being quick to recognize a dangerous situation, Doc Ball summoned two passersby, and they got the man into his front room clinic. After securing neck braces and making the man feel as comfortable as possible for a broken neck, Doc Ball found out just what happened.

It seemed the doctor had a runaway team of horses. Their fright was caused by the humming sound of a quail that had literally flown out from under the horses. They, in turn, ran off the road and over a falling tree before he could check them. This, in turn, tossed the doctor backward over the hack's backseat, causing him to land on his head and break his neck. Knowing about broken necks and what would happen if something is not done pretty quick, the doctor grabbed a handful of hair and held his own head up and in place, which wasn't easy. Luckily, the hack wasn't demolished. The team settled down, and the doctor continued down the road, holding his head up with his hand. He arrived in front of Doc Ball's clinic which was a few miles away.

Here's another story about Doc Ball. In those days, cleanliness was next to godliness. Doc Ball was a firm believer in this frontier quotation no matter how messy the situation got. Oftentimes, the kind doctor needed to have his buggy repaired or the wheels greased, a service provided

OLD GEORGE

Drovers were always driving cattle either in to town or out. At the edge of town, there was a small trap (pasture) which had a good fence around it and a stock tank. It seemed this little trap was right handy to penstock for the night. Since there was no visible house in sight or an owner around, some drovers put stock in the pasture without asking. So the sheriff took over, kinda like, and made a trap out of this trap, so to speak. The sheriff told the drovers who passed through, "Stranger, you go ahead and out your cattle in there. If a big N——o comes around, you just tell 'im the sheriff told you to do that." Not too many N——s owned property around these parts in those days. It seemed that some overbearing fellows would take advantage of the old N——o, whose name was George. So the sheriff took it on himself to collect pasturage and turn it over to old George.

ALL DRIED UP

Cattle on the ranch generally took up all a cattle owner's time. There were weak cows, sick cows, and d——d cows, and then there were dry cows. These cows were what was known as barren because they did not breed and bring back a calf. Now, calves are what make the wheels turn on a cow ranch. When shipping time comes, it's time for a roundup, a little operation that is headquartered in the most wide-open spaces.

For the roundup, the drovers station themselves around the herd, whether it numbers a hundred or few thousand. The top horse is the drover who rides into this milling mess and cuts out the dry critters, or whatever else he is after. Generally, dry cows can be spotted easily no matter how the dust blows. Ordinarily, since they aren't nursing a calf, dry cows are in pretty good shape. They are slick, shiny, and fat. Any fool, though, can look at a cow's milk department and tell whether or not she has a calf. But then there's always room left for doubt.

The top horse had arrived in one of those rooms. He wasn't sure if he had spotted a dry cow or not. This dry un had all the markings of a dry un, and it out top horse to shifting gears to cut her from the herd. Well, the top horse always gets the job done no matter what so that critter ended up in the cuts. But that critter was just as determined to get back in the herd—no matter what. The boys holding that cut were just as good as the top horse. The top horse had plenty of good hands and mounts. They could cut grasshoppers from a locust cloud. The antsy cow settled down and resigned to simply bide her time with the rest of the dry cows. Anyway, the boys had other things to worry about.

A fellow by the name of Lilley happened to be on the cutting edge of the herd. This was where the cutting—and the other cutting—was not too dull. Lilley's horse was just about the cash in his chips. The top horse might have raised the bugle too many times. Lilley was an old-time cowman, not a cowboy. He knew about that there dry that was straining the minds of mice and men. This cow was pretty well surrounded, but back at the herd, where Lilley as working, something else was taking place: a great big old calf.

Lilley knew about this big old calf and just simply let him slip by out the herd. Of course, at that precise moment, the top horse told Lilley that, "By golly, he had let one get by!" So at that precise moment, Lilley rode up alongside the

OF PEACHES AND PEPPERMINT

Sam Bass was an outlaw. The cedar breaks around these parts played an intriguing part in Sam's life. This was in Caddo, Texas. He had found a rock cave somewhere in Mid-Calf Gap. There was a little store that set beside the trail that led north. This store was located some miles farther on that Sam's cave. Sam liked that little store. But the sheriff at the country seat sure would have liked to put Sam behind bars. In other words, doing so would put a feather in the sheriff's hat, so to speak, or even under it. Yes, the sheriff knew that Sam Bass was a bad man, a gunman with a pretty good shot. He was the type of fellow who would bet on his own horse, the Denton mare. Word had it that Sam was hanging out around the little store, so Mr. Sheriff sent his most trusted deputy—the sheriff had trained him himself—to this little store to bring Mr. Bad Man into his justice. After all, hadn't Sam hurt the sheriff's right arm? Didn't that bandage prove it?

In this little store I was telling you about, the storekeeper served the good along with the bad, and he generally respected both kinds. Maybe it was honor among thieves. So it was that Mr. Bass hitched his horse to the store's gallery post. Sam wanted to do some shopping inside. Sam loved these newfangled commodities, especially canned peaches. He'd ride ten miles for them. In fact, he rode a good many miles to this here little store just to procure a can.

What the deputy didn't see when he rode up and entered the store was Sam. But the lawman had seen Sam's horse tied outside. Sam was behind a high counter procuring a can of these luscious goods. The lawman couldn't wait for his eyes to adjust to the dimness, and that's when Sam made his move. The young lawman was now standing at the front counter with his back to Sam. Getting into such a position was sure not what the sheriff had taught him.

Sam approached and lifted the lawman's pistol. He had an open can of them brand-new-type peaches, and, like I said, sure did like them. But not only that, Sam was game too but them like everybody else. The lawman, however, had gotten in the way. The deputy didn't move when he realized Sam was behind him; he just watched Sam go around him and seat himself on the countertop and place that big can of peaches alongside his leg.

Sam sliced into a peach with his long-bladed sheath knife. With its point, he placed a peach chunk between a row of white teeth. Between chunks, Sam mentioned to the deputy just how good the peaches were and talked about the ingenuity of the peach-canning trade. The deputy was all in agreement. Sam then noticed a big jar of peppermint stick candy sitting on a shelf. Sam mentioned to the storekeeper that the deputy should join him. The storekeeper then placed the big jar of candy before the standing lawman.

Sam told the storekeeper he wanted to treat the deputy. When Sam had a bite of peach, the lawman would have a bite of peppermint candy stick that resided in that big glass jar. Of course, Sam's long-braded knife could whittle peaches down to bite sizes. That can of peaches against that big glass jar of peppermint stick candy bad odds. The storekeeper then dismissed himself to his duties of minding the store, for he knew very well that he can hold a lot of fruit and the jar held a lot of peppermint sticks.

A few hours later, the storekeeper found the correct amount of money on the counter for one big can of peaches—and 150 peppermint sticks! The storekeeper trusted that Sam had counted the sticks to arrive at the cost. The storekeeper also found a mighty sick lawman setting on the floor and leaning against the counter.

When the storekeeper put the much-distressed deputy on his horse for the ride back to the county seat, he noticed the deputy's coat pockets were filled with peppermint stick candy. Well, the storekeeper figured it weren't none of his business or concern, for Sam just might be watching from somewhere.

GETTING RAILROADED

Shipping cattle to market involves two steps: driving the cattle on a trail that leads to the railhead, then loading them on a train that will take them to another distant market, such as Chicago. The first trip up the trail was a test against raw nature for both young and old alike. Being on the railroad, though, was worse. Railroading cattle was not only a test of man against animal but also drovers against trainmen and that man-made, fast-moving, smoke-belching, whistle-blowing iron horse. All you have to do is think of all the meanings of the word "railroad," and you'll get a better picture of what it was like for the cow drovers. You can railroad—that is, transport, something—such as cattle or you can railroad, meaning make hasty judgments about somebody. Both happened in the business of railroading cattle. Which was worse, the trail or the train? Well, that's a tough one for them Yale scholars to go figure. I'll present the facts and let you decide for yourself.

A fellow might say all the bugaboo between the railroad men and the working trail drovers started when the first critter was prodded into one of those railroad cattle cars. The word prodded might be a little weak because some of the critters still wanted to get back south the best way they knew how, which certainly was not aboard a locomotive. For starters, the railroad men didn't like the way drovers yelled and gave out short, little commands. The railroad men, however, didn't realize the drovers lived in a fast-moving world; that is, fast-moving cattle that had fast-moving minds and fast-moving horses too. The drovers had to yell, and maybe just one short, loud time, because one time might be the only time they had. The drover made every single move and command count for it could be his last.

Actually, the problems the railbirds had to put up with was their own making. The cattle car doors had to be lined up with the loading chute opening; and if the two weren't lined perfectly, the drovers stepped in and made them that way. Drovers had to insure against any kind of crack or opening in which a leg or foot could get caught. If there was an opening like that, the train would have to be moved either forward or backward, which, of course, caused the brakeman much lantern-waving. And as you'd expect, the lantern-waving brakeman didn't appreciate the drovers horning in on his job. The drovers d——n sure didn't want his job; they just didn't want the stock crippled up. Drovers didn't like to see suffering critters, either good or bad.

With three thousand head going to market, it would take some time to shape up and load a hundred carloads. Each car loaded about thirty-five heads depending on what kind of cattle they were. Overloading a car caused plenty of trouble. Thus, the cattle owner might have to secure several trains or how many he could get at that time.

The drover who goes with the cattle train looks after the welfare of all the loaded stock. Every so often, he must make his way atop the moving cars to inspect the stock. If one was down, the drover would have to make his way to where the critter was and proceed to get him up. The term "tail up" is precisely what it means. A bison rises to his feet from behind. A horse gets to its feet from the front. When a cow starts up, it uses its tail in a like manner. Generally, all that is needed is giving the downed critter enough room to get up by keeping the rest of the herd far enough away from the cow's hind legs. A drover always carried a prod pole for this purpose. Most trains furnished these prod poles. This was where the drover inherited the name cowpuncher. He used this pole to prod the cattle back and give the downed one a chance to get up. If the critter didn't get up, the drover made his way to it and tailed it up. By taking hold of the tail, roping the cow's neck, and using no. 64 jumper strength and a few heavy words, a drover could put a nine-hundred-pound steer back on its feet. Mind you, all this was done among stock with long, shiny horns that would fight an elephant bull and while the train was moving down the tracks at top speed.

By morning, most of the cattle were what they called roadbroke. They had spent the night learning to stand while the train moved or rolled around a curve. The cows would discover that they could retain their balance by leaning in the opposite direction of a curve. Once this learning took place, the drover could bed down in the caboose.

The weather might be a shade cold, but the train crew might have a fire going in the coal stove. There also might be coffee in a black pot letting out a delicious aroma. If the crew was congenial, they would offer coffee to the drover before he stretched out for a bit of shut-eye. But some of these trainmen didn't offer. Well, the drover did bring the smell of fresh bison and other foul odors into the train crew's heaven. And some of the crew also remembered all that trail herd yelling back at the loading chutes. Some of the trainmen though were just plain bastards. Well, the drover made it a point to surround this type with all his smelly "blessings." And if the drover wasn't offered coffee, he simply helped himself. If the crew didn't make room for him, he pushed them over. You see, the drover's boss had paid for this train, its steam, its wheels, its lanterns, its coffee, and also its space. The drover was his boss's representative. The boss did the same thing.

All the equipment went with the drover; for example, may be an extra saddle horse. The saddle and sugans were stored somewhere in the caboose,. Most of the train crew took their place up in the "pupeilo," the roof above the main car. Long, wide benches ran the length of the car, and little compartments on each end held train equipment. The coal stove had its place in the middle of the floor. The drover took up one bench. On a row of wooden wall pegs, he hung his yellow slicker, maybe his belted pistol, a rifle in its scabbard, his saddle, and his favorite ketch rope. The prod poles were stored in each cattle car.

The same train crew didn't complete the whole trip. At certain points, which were called division points, one crew would get off and another crew would get on. The fresh crewmen would be greeted with this dirty, smelly drover stretched out asleep on one of their benches—right by the stove that would hatch out a setting of banty eggs. When all that heat rose up in the pupeilo, there would follow a fresh bison-smelling, stall-smelling, leathery fragrance that accompanied it. Yes sirree, that there train crew with all their finery didn't deserve those stinking old cows. Why one of them complained how his wife had cooked his steak that morning because of the smell!

Moreover, when the train has to take on water, the cattle have to take on water too, and such an occurrence reminded the train crew of the original chute loading with all that yelling since the drovers would have to unload and reload the cattle. A few more days of this and with that dumb cowpuncher giving out both orders and odors, well... And some crewmen remembered just how this drover felt about his cattle. Some of them might turn in at night with black eyes and marked-up faces. The drover got his work done no matter what, that's for sure. Moreover, one thing the train crew did not see was this smelly thing take a drink of firewater while on the job. This was a mystery the crew aimed to leave alone.

To be fair, the train crews weren't always to blame, and the drover was sometimes responsible for his own predicaments. The towns train passed through were little one-cow farming places. Most drovers, by far, liked to whop it up, nearby, just not on the job. The red-eyed bottle helped drovers to whop it up at the stops in the larger towns, where fast women and fast panhandlers added to fast whopping. Of course, after a while, the drover would find out he had been duped. That's when he checked the cylinders in his hog-leg pistol and went hunting which could get him into a heap of trouble.

But the drovers had a right to complain about the train and its crew, for they even got in the drover's way out on the trail. The drover always knew those d——n trains were his enemy. One drover had said trains were like the Indians, they belched black smoke and always screamed at the drop of a feather. Oh, that train whistle! It came on especially when a herd was bunched close to the tracks. The train and its whistle would send the herd running over vast sections of prairie land. Then the drover could see the d——n laughing faces of the train crew. Yeah, that hole in their faces made a good target! Sometimes when the drovers were moving horses down the trail near the tracks, the engineer couldn't wait to pull that steam valve. No kind of mother tornado could catch those horses. Some drovers just don't cotton to that, and you can't blame them. Maybe a few shots ricocheting off that gig just might send those trainmen a message.

Yep, the tension was strong enough that some drovers figured it was always open season for trains. At night, many lights brightened up those passenger cars. From nearby boarding house porches, a drover could shoot out those lights. The drover's partner—his pard—who also had recollections of horses or cattle stampeding out the corral on account of an amusing steam whistle, would often take up where his pard left off. Pretty soon, when trains passed through certain towns, the crew would turn out all the lights. Those on board sure would have second thoughts about striking a match!

Most cattle owners hired a drover who was down to earth, so to speak. She might be taking care of some stocks and young'uns also. Most cow bosses' sentiments pointed in that same direction. The bosses and the drovers knew right from wrong. That was the way their wives were, and they brought children up that way too. But sometimes a fellow just has to stand up and be counted, that's for d——n sure, for better or for worse. For example, those Casey-Jones specials, for the trainmen, brought their eats in little tin boxes. The drover's life was far from being a boxed-meal kind of life. Drovers had no place for such things as tin box treats and no one to fix them. Drovers either did without or good trainmen would share a bit of their grub with the drover.

But most of the time, the drover had to provide for himself, which he did at stops. Little towns scattered up and down the railroad earned the name of jerkwater towns, and they generally had an eating establishment nestled close by. The drover didn't take long in locating these places—and it didn't take long for him to learn what kind of time the train ran on. If the brakeman told him there would be plenty of time, the drover would order ham and eggs—if the trainman liked him. If he didn't, the drover could be caught in horseshoe-bending fist because he would see the train pulling out before the ham and eggs ever got to him! Then he'd have to run like a striped baboon in his high-heeled boots and try to hook onto that caboose. Such an experience the drover wouldn't soon forget. At the next water stop, the drover would single out the trainman. Buckling on his pistol or cradling his rifle, the drover again would ask the trainman just how long would be the stop. The trainman soon understood just what that drover was really thinking. If the gun pointed at the trainman didn't help him estimate the time more precisely, his memory of going through towns like Hays or Dodge City and having to put out all the train's lights might. As you might have guessed, some railroad men retired at an early age. Like I said, sometimes a fellow just has to stand up for himself.

Of course, the drover knew that not all trainmen were mortal enemies. There were some big cows' outfits that owned trains, and they thought they owned the tracks too. Train-owning outfits could be worse than some trainmen. In the cattle business, there was always movement—be it on the trail or on the tracks—to get a herd to market, and competition could be fierce. In some cases, a classic trail boss would have his outfit drive at night to get around and ahead of another cattle owner's herd. Staying ahead took a lot of doing and was a hardship on both stock and men—especially when the railroad was involved. One drover told a story about a giant of an outfit in Texas that owned a train. This outfit, however, couldn't beat the drover and his outfit's herd to the loading chutes in Abilene. So the train-owning outfit had to be second behind the ATSF train, which the drover's outfit had procured.

But those train owners didn't like being second. On the roaring trip to Chicago, their rip-snorting battle wagon with wheels put itself about a tongue's-length behind the ATSF caboose. At night, the drover watched the ATSF brakeman standing on the caboose's platform tossing out flares in the middle of the tracks to let the engineer in the train behind him know (as if he didn't) there was another train ahead of him. I should have said running ninety to nothing for dear life! That poor brakeman wanted to get back home in one piece! Now, anyone who's got an ounce of sense knows that trains just can't pass on a single track.

But the engineer in the second train must have thought, Like hell, there might be. Right here on the Atchison, Topeka, and Santa Fe there might be.

After all was said and done, getting even was easier than outing a stampede to boil. The drover told the brakeman to save his flares. The two front lights of that second train danced around on the big brass bell, which was outlined in front of the big black smokestack, seemed to the drover to be a mighty fine target. He spat a heavy bullet squarely on the round dome. It shed off the concave and put a long furrow alongside the belching stack. A little smoke trickled out. He followed this shot with another in case the engineer couldn't hear too well. The engineer evidently couldn't because he put on more steam and pulled up closer. Well, after the drover shot out the lights on that highballing battle wagon, the brakeman and his crew put out all their lights so those in the second train wouldn't have an easy target. It didn't take long for the brakeman and drover to hear compressed air come on. Steel wheels could be heard gritting against the steel tracks. "It sure is dark back thar no!"

After the stock was delivered in Chicago, then, of course, was the long trip back. At the end of the line, the drover gathered up his horses, packs, and headed back down to Texas on horseback. Sometimes, these trips were as gritty as the train trips north.

The territory was about what the word means; it wasn't a state, and it wasn't strong on law and order. The federal marshals from Fort Smith scouted the insides for intruders. Sometimes they caught them, and sometimes they didn't.

The drover had made camp alongside the Canadian River. He awoke early the next morning, but not by his own choosing.

A pistol with a big bore was staring him in the eye. Some other forms were standing behind his gun. Of course, the drover gave up immediately. He sure didn't like anyone getting the drop of him though. But the silver stars hanging from leather vests made him feel a little better about the situation. It was not until one lawman found several thousand dollars in the drover's saddlebags that the drover began to feel like these marshals might try to "railroad" him for stealing, but carrying that much money was nothing new. He had packed cattle money all over for years. Mr. Black always gave him receipts for the horses. After the drover showed the lawmen the waybills and bills of sale for the cattle and horses, it became evident to the lawmen that the drover wasn't the fellow they were after. The horse brands matched, the money matched, and the drover matched the thinking of the marshals.

The drover then made coffee for them all, and the marshals told him there was a bad hombre roaming around the countryside. Seems this hombre had killed a deputy down south of here, and there was a reward out for him.

This activity was enticing to lawmen, especially here in the territory. The deputy had been transporting this hombre and another prisoner to the federal prison up north. This hombre had managed to slip his feet out his boots and therefore freed the shackles around them. Riding in the hack, the deputy couldn't keep his eyes on two prisoners all the time; and anyway they were supposed to be chained hand and foot. In freeing himself from the leg irons, this outlaw was able to move forward and remove the deputy's pistol and shot him in the back.

Bad Un was quick, all right. He was quick to grab the team's lines while still chained to the other prisoner. Being handcuffed to the other man, he still had problems, but not for long. Old Bad Un couldn't find the keys to the handcuffs. What he didn't know was that the keys were at the prison office a long ways off. But he soon figured that out. So he just shot his attached companion to death. Using an axe that was fastened under the hack seat, he cut off the dead prisoner's hand and took off on the team of horses. These lawmen thus were checking every nook and cranny north of here. The marshals had no second thoughts about running Bad Un into the ground.

The drover mentioned that he would not linger too long on the trail back to the home range. The drover found out later that the lawmen had trailed the killer to his brother's farm. There in his house the two put up a gun battle with the marshals, but the long arm of the law quelled its offenders.

THE PORCH

The drover remembered several incidents that took place along the trail north. One such occurrence was something to write home about. Mr. Black and his men had camped a few miles from the headquarters of a big ranch. The outfit's cooking supplies were low, so the drover took a wagon, and he and the cook drover, over to this place. They were greeted handsomely, as all were treated in those days. Of course, they received the supplies the cook needed. Since it was near noon and they weren't going to turn down any noontime grub, they stayed over. This was by no means a small ranch. The two put their team away and hung around the main house till the dinner bell rang. The drover noticed about forty, maybe fifty saddle horses that were even ground hitched. The long ranch house porch was filled with drovers a setting, leaning, laying, playing cards, shooting dice, or just plain smoking. This was something unusual around a cow outfit. The drover figured these men were doing what he and the cook were doing: waiting on the dinner bell. The cook thought about all them elbows putting away all that grub. The drover then figured all those drovers were waiting for the ranch wagon to pull out. They were, perhaps, waiting on a roundup job. Of course, the ranch would not hire all the drovers. What was strange about the whole thing was when the grub bell rang, they all went and caught fresh horses and then unsaddled the ones that were tied to trees, fences, and posts; they then saddled the fresh horses and tied them back to trees, fences, and posts. Then the men all went inside for grub call. After the meal, they returned to the ranch's long porch and picked up where they had left off: setting, leaning, laying, playing cards, shooting dice, or just plain smoking.

STORIES FROM OUT WHERE THE COWS ARE

One still, warm night, the drover was standing his guard. Three more drovers were setting their horses around the bedded herd. These were the last guards, midnight till daybreak. Another drover, Emiline, had joined him. Emiline was stating a plain fact, and the drover very well knew it. The other guards were in quite a pell-mell. They were riding around talking to the cattle to try to calm them for they were beginning to rise up from the bed-ground. What was taking places was slow-motion version of a stampede.

Emiline explained later, "Me and Charley rode down the river earlier that night, and we rode up to this house where a piano was playing out some awful ripsaw chords. We helloed the house, then I asked the piano player would it be all right if the piano stayed silent until the Muleshoe herd moved out."

Something happened a few days later, and it could have happened at least a thousand times. But once was enough. The drover, on trail drives, had in addition to his mounts (saddle horses), a couple of inefficient horses. Inefficient means they don't know too much—and they could mean either drovers or broncs. Let me explain for those who might not know about the training and drilling of a reliable saddle horse. Plain and simple, there are two kinds of horses: saddle horses and cow horses. These two can be worlds apart. The drover catches his mount to use that particular day, maybe on the outside circle of the herd. Well, the outside circle can be a long way off. So the drover dabs his loop on that fifteen-hand sorrel or black and head out there. He'd be looking at a long day of brushy miles. This was just the place to get a jugheaded bronc to recognize just how long a day was.

Well, the drover and Emiline were on the outside circle looking for strays. Emiline was riding a young jugheaded bronc who cold jawed and ran off down the river bottom. The drover tried to help his old friend, Emiline, break the jughead. Finally out in open ground, they just let the critter run. But things get in the way. One thing is trees. Showing a young bronc how to be bridlewise takes a heap of showing, not only to the one being shown but also to the one doing the showing. When the bronc started running, about the only thing to do was keep him from firing dead center into one of those gentle trees. So the drover rode along trying to keep him out rocks and such.

When a bronc is running cold jawed, he is not too concerned about what lays ahead, only in trying to run out from under that weight on his back or make it disappear. About that time, the darn thing stepped in a hole. The horse went down and Emiline couldn't get clear because his foot had gotten caught in the stirrup. The weight of the horse drove Emiline's booted foot into the ground. His pard was quick to dismount and hold the struggling bronc from getting to its feet. He was able to calm down the horse, undo the saddle cinches, and free the downed rider. Well, the drover resaddled the bronc and helped Emiline back on, and they rode to the nearest house. They recognized the range where they were. Emiline then pointed out to the drover that they were arriving at the house where the piano player had played all night a few days ago. Emiline, who had been the one who had, in a painstaking way, asked the piano player to quit playing that piano. He recalled saying that the sound would likely scare the herd off the bedground and send them fixing for parts unknown.

Emiline's foot had swollen, and the boot had to be cut off. This is something no drover wants done no matter what, even if a bone might be broken. That's when the piano player brought out a high-top woman's shoe. Like most drovers, Emiline had small feet, so the shoe was likely to fit. The piano player, with a sly grin on her face, put the shoe on the twisted foot and laced it up. As the two men prepared to head back to the cow wagon, the piano player mentioned to the cripple that that was the shoe she had played piano with!

The drovers had moved the herd somewhere near the Kansas border. Emiline needed a doctor's touch for his foot. The wagon boss thought there might be a settlement a few miles off. But sometimes a few miles turn into a few days out here. Emiline and the drover set out again on horseback. It took them all day long to get in sight of the little town. Emiline fared as best he could and rode with his leg hooked around the saddle horn to keep his busted foot from throbbing too much. All the while, the high-top ladies' shoe was showing. The two located a sawbones, and this doctor patched up Emiline's foot and put him to rest in his house.

Emiline's pard would ride back to the wagon that night. It wasn't that easy, that is, getting back to the wagon. The night was as black as pitch, and very few stars were visible. The drover knew he was riding in circles but couldn't do too much about it.

All horsemen know if a horse is given his head, he will go home to the feed bag. The drover knew all this. But right now the horse more than likely wanted to go back to Texas. That sure wasn't where the drover's sugans were. But a horse can smell water, cows, and other horses. Other horses were what the drover was counting on. So they plowed on. They had been riding a long time on the trail, and the drover's mount was getting leg weary. Crossing a brushy draw, the drover's horse came to a halt. It was so dark the drover couldn't see his horse's ears. A little spurring and clucking by the drover didn't even get the horse to move on. Then it dawned on the drover: the horse was listening. The drover could hear nothing though. The horse finally moved out and down the draw. Thirty minutes later, they arrived at the wagon—one tired horse and one tired drover. But this was not the only time the drover had gotten turned around.

The Choctaw Range was nothing to sneeze at. One time, the drover was after a big old three-year-old steer out on this range. This steer was a bunch quitter and wanted desperately to get back to Texas and a dead run wasn't quick enough. It's not unbecoming for these critters to evade a drover for miles. They can be very cunning. They will lay up in thick brush, keep their heads down, and not make a sound. They lie on the ground keeping their heads down, and a careless drover will ride right by them and never know of the critter's presence. An old cow horse will though. A horse cannot verbally speak, but the messages he sends out are by the way of ears. Sometimes these old ranch horses will get on a hunt too, and if the rider gives his mount some rein and lets him go, the horse will flush the old bugger out the brush.

This old bugger of a steer the drover was after had led many a chase away from the herd. Time changed, the sun changed, and the surroundings changed. Finally, the drover roped the critter and put side lines on him; that is, the front foot is tied to the back foot with a good length of gentle rope. All this does is slow a critter down a trifle. Now, the steer had Texas on its mind, the drover had the chuck wagon on his mind: the one with the most determination would win.

The drover sure was set on winning. His next step was to drive back to where they had come from. The direction should have been a fact, but which way was it? The drover had gotten turned around. It was some miles away. The steer, the horse, and the rider made their way opposite the sun. Somewhere up ahead there ought to be a three-thousand-head trail herd. Anybody should be able to see a herd that size. It was way past grub time, watering time too. That's when the old bugger sniffed the air and tried to take off. But the sidelines held him. The drover knew the old bugger had smelled water. So the three headed in that direction. Leastwise, that d——n critter was worth five dollars.

In a little while, they rode out in a creek bottom. The country began to fan out. The drover remembered crossing a river before. Maybe this one they had come to was the same one; it was as crooked as a dog's hind leg. They watered up. The drover found a crossing, but on the other side, they found company. Naw, the drover didn't care much about Indians. Sometimes where there's one there might be a bunch back in the brush. After looking for holes in the brush, the drover decided this Indian was a loner. Since the steer, who had been so rambunctious earlier, seemed to be at home grazing on the short grass, the drover thought, Well, I'll try and talk a spell. He then asked, "Have you seen a heap big cow head?" No use going into numbers right now.

No sound.

Well, I'll try another line. "Have you seen many horses?" the drover said slowly, as he shaded his eyes, looked in the direction of the distant hills, then pointed to his horse. This time, he did get some response, but he didn't like the way the Indian was staring at his horse.

No sound.

The drover realized the Indian didn't know how to talk, only use sign language, but he himself didn't savvy none of that. Then the drover looked at the Indian's horse, which was a darn good one. A good horse just stands out, like a polished jewel in bright sunlight. Wonder where he got 'im at? I wonder... The drover liked the horse so much he wanted to try to trade for him. But there was language barrier; besides, if he did make a trade, the Indian might steal the horse back that night, and the drover figured it looked like he was already going to have to sleep on his saddle blanket. In fact, he figured he had better tie old Rocket to his arm tonight, so he changed his mind and decided he would just stay in the creek and head that way. The Indian then continued on across the water.

After riding many more miles, the drover began keeping his eyes on the steer, for the drover knew the steer would eventually give away the location. Soon enough, the steer tossed his head and let out a bellow, then started bearing off to the side; the side lines still kept him from running. The drover just let his horse follow. Once the group got out the creek bottom and climbed up a low hill, the drover spotted the herd. There was the blue smoke from the cook's fire! Then the drover could smell food. It sure smelled good! The drover's appetite was what they called "caved in." He let the steer graze on the tall grass outside the camp along with his ground-hitched horse then strolled over to where the cook was tending pots.

"What yea doin' in thar?" he heard the cook remark as he took a black dutch oven off the glowing coals. When the cook lifted the oven's hot lid, a big bullfrog jumped out. The drover had to hide a laugh. The hoodlum probably was the culprit. The cold bacon and biscuit tasted mighty good. The saddle horse grazed beside the big old bugger steer, who was now gentler than a milk cow and acting just as if nothing in the worlds ever happened.

TAKIN' CARE OF BUSINESS—AND PLEASURE

I

Owning your own cows makes a heap of a difference—that is, dollars-and-cents wise. In his early days, the drover picked up baby calves; the ones that were born on the trail and left behind, for they would not be able to make the trip. He left these little critters with Uncle Charley. When these little critters became big, they would be put in with a herd going north. They also wore the drover's brand. Now, it takes two years for a steer to grow into trail size—that means market size. As the years increased, so did the herd. As long as there was a trail herd, there would be baby ones, lame ones, and not too lame ones. Thus, the increase in years brought on an increase in the number of cattle, which, in turn, increased the need for more fine grassland.

The Chain C Cattle Ranch lay south. The country was cedar breaks, hills, mountains, and rocky creeks, draws, and just plain washouts. The Chain C Cattle Company wanted to sell off all its range stock and lease its land to outfits that needed the space. The owner of the Chain C Cattle Company knew such a transaction would be worth the money because the cattle he owned were wild. He decided to sell his cattle by range delivery. Range delivery means that a cattle owner sells his stock by head count, but buyers do the gathering—in this case where the hills, mountains, and rocky creeks, draws, and washouts are. But this kind of terrain can hinder a heap in getting a high head count. And a high head count make a heap of difference in this type of cow trade, especially when the buyer puts up his own stock as collateral to a bank to pull off the deal. Both sides, the owner and the bank, might end up grinning from head to toe. If the buyer fails, the ranch would take back its cattle and the bank would take its money, and the drover would have to start all over again.

But sometimes a big honcho doesn't know just how some other folks operate. These brush poppers (another word for drovers, especially those who search out strays) can hang on like a five-year drought. In the Muleshoe days, the drover learned a whole lot about this south country. So they loaded up their gear and set out. "They" included two-pack horses, twenty heads of saddle stock, the drover, Boss Martin, and Bill Gauge. They savvied cedar breaks, rock mountains, and wild cattle that just loved to be there. They would be gone for three months. So to keep the home fires burning, a three months' supply of firewood was cut for the womenfolk staying behind.

On the trip down to Chain C country, all signs of cattle were investigated. This meant unpacking, making camp, and putting the saddle horse stock where they would stay put, for it's bad enough hunting wild cattle; hunting your own saddle horses, for which a drover doesn't get paid, is something else. Looking for cow signs is one way a fellow learns the lay of the land. This procedure can be a problem though. Sometimes these cow signs showed that the cattle were just passing through; other times the cattle would show signs of holing up in a little green valley then moving on. The men found a large number of watering places. If these signs stayed put, then there would be water around. That's what the men wanted to do. Once you locate the water holes then things usually start adding up, like the size of the range here. That would be a start. What the men didn't want to do was scatter the herd again. The drover figured that there was around a hundred heads watering around this water hole. The cattle were grazing in those little secluded valleys rimmed with brush and rocky cliffs. These were conventional places for all wild cattle and for those who wanted to be wild. These were the cattle who didn't like stock markets, saddle horses, and especially them two-legged critters setting on top.

The creeks ran between hills and mountains. In hot weather, the water dried up in the shallows, leaving holes of water up and down the creek. Sometimes these holes were miles apart. These were places the drover was going to use to break up this cow convention. The drovers put in a water trap. There were plenty of bossies watering around here. The drovers pitched the camp on a knoll on the side of the mountain, which provided a clear view up and down the creek. Clear, cool water gushed out of rocks here. That was another good reason for setting up camp here. This water ran on down the mountain in the opposite direction then it fanned out across a little valley and into a main creek. That valley was where the saddle stock was pastured.

The water traps were pretty easy to build. Around most of the holes of water the creek banks rose up; high enough that an animal couldn't climb out. All that needed to be done was to put stout poles across both ends and a pole gate in each middle. From up on the knoll, the men could spot cattle coming from both directions. Whatever direction they came from, the opposite pole gate could be closed before the stock got to it. The drovers would wait till all the cattle were inside then bar up the gate they came through. The job was real easy—if the cows didn't get the wind of the poler. They didn't call them brush masters and bugger bears for nothing.

The drovers didn't trap the first day; they just counted the cattle and let them sniff at the new pole fence. That morning, the men counted about thirty heads and that evening about forty. The cows all had big calves. That made the drover count his chickens before they were hatched, and he didn't want to drop no eggs! The drovers also knew a few heads, which also came in from the same direction, watered at night. That made another thought start running through the men's heads. The creek banks were still quite high on up along the creek. So they moved a ways and put in another pole fence that was good and stout, maybe even bulletproof. What the drovers had running through their heads was killing several birds with the same rock—Cedar Creek rock.

The drovers closed the front gate that next morning so the cattle wouldn't be able to get to the water. The drovers didn't get much sleeping done the following night for the thirsty cattle bawling all night. By daylight, the drover counted about sixty heads, all with big old cow-egg calves. By midday, the whole bunch had moved back to the range to graze. That day, the gate was let down. Now the drovers would see what dollar signs really looked like. As the sun reached its zenith and started its decline, the men spotted some color trailing up through the brush. From the knoll, they would tell these critters were in a thirsty walk. There were about sixty heads with big old calves, and some were big yearlings that were still claiming their mama better, for a big old range bull, if he didn't want to go, generally hooked the cows back toward the home range.

Up until now, these cows hadn't missed many water-drinking periods, so they started drinking like the water was going out of style. Then they started laying down with the waterlog, which was just what the drovers wanted: get them ripsnorting full, so maybe there would be no ripsnorting running. The men then pulled the poles across the opening, which changed their minds of the old bossies about lying down just yet. The other gate was let down, and the herd was moved to the back side. Some of the old bossies sure had fire in their eyes when they spotted them two-legged critters on the ground! Why, they even charged the fence they were behind! The drover thus remembered the cows that were in the guilty party because they were the little jewels that would scatter the herd once they were taken outside the fence. The men set the trap for another operation that night. When daylight exposed itself on this little scene, of course minds started getting brighter. The drovers worked this trap until no more cattle went into the water. More traps would be built father away from this range. The drover believed he had them all on this side: three bulls with fire in their eyes, 150 cows some with fire in their eyes, and the bunch of wild-eyed yearlings.

When a fellow parted with a dollar out here in those days, it was easier for him to catch his shadow then to try to get that money back. In other words, the drover had a whole lot of trouble getting the bank to back an operation like this. In retrospect though the bank was holding his cattle as collateral, but losing them would hurt. And the drover didn't need any more hunting experience. Neither did the bank.

What happened was that the bank initially would not lend the drover the money to gather Chain C cattle on a head-count basis. It's risky business to listen to fat chair seats who really don't know much about cows. No, you are not going to get that sort off their fats to even look. Remember, bankers' butts straddle plush, thick chairs. But the drovers' butts set on anything that pops up. That's good, sound business. But Mr. Ward was a banker who was not like most bankers, and he saw something else. He saw that this drover was a good cowman. Mr. Ward was a banker all right, but he overrode his co-worker's decision to deny the drovers a loan. Mr. Ward would let the drover gather the Chain C stock with his money. And gather them they did.

What made the drovers start popping was when they drover 150 cows with two calves each and five baloney bulls down Main Street and put them in the N———o's wire trap. They stayed in town just long enough; of course, with the help of banker Ward to open an account in this bank. Mr. Ward still wanted his money to stay close.

What the drover didn't know were the thoughts of the high-class banker, who had initially turned him down for the loan. The drover walked on by through the business section, where that little high-class, owl-faced sucker sat. But the Owl Face had been the first one in the bank to see the herd coming down the street. He was tugging on his goatee, listening to the drover's spurs jingle out a happy rhythm as he thumped by his desk. Apparently, someone was going to do better than a big un, this big un figured, so he decided he should lend the drover a hand. The big un approached the drover using the most conducive, exuberant talk a big un banker could muster.

It never occurred to the drover that someone in such a so-called "good position" could ever be so obsessed with wanting to put him down or so happy to foreclose on him. This big un obviously didn't take into consideration that the drover was a cowman and that the trail—the drovers' office—was a proving ground. A drover learns soon that there is a certain breed of man that will beat its own mother, and he watches out for that type, whether he's on the range or in town.

In short order, the drover located a cattle buyer. Those cattle in the N——o's little wire trap wouldn't be there long. Right now, he was more interested in getting back to gathering Chain C wild cows with two calves (a yearling and a calf that is still nursing). The drover figured there might be some eight hundred heads down in that hellish land, and he was going to gather them. He sort of liked the hollow look on Owl Face there at the bank and would love to see it again.

II

The drovers set up their camp five miles from their last camp. That particular day, Boss Martin and Bill Gauge had plenty of luck—the kind of luck that is both good and bad. Stock in the cedar breaks is bad luck. One needed cow-hunting luck. Today, their cow-hunting luck wasn't so good, so they started using ketch ropes. By the time the sun set behind that hellish land, there were nine bossies tied to nine gentle trees. The yearlings and calves had run off. They would be back. But they also had two big steers with broken necks.

That night in camp, the three drovers were deciding how to add those mine bossies to the herd. Today, the animal lovers' right associations sure would march had the drovers' plans about handling wild cattle been revealed. They didn't have any rich fathers-in-law or rich uncles to fortify their means. Handling cattle was the livelihood of all three drovers. What the animal rights people don't do is gather these cattle. They don't know, and they don't need to know drovers go about their business. They just use a ratchet jaw.

There are several ways of making things go in the same direction to get wild cattle to market. The total is three: horse, cow, and, of course, rider. The cattle that were for sale needed to be sold; and a loan needed to be paid back, especially when a good friend like Mr. Ward had lent the money to purchase the cows in the first place. Getting nine heads of grown stock back to the herd shouldn't be a big deal.

After an all-night stay with a tree, the old bossies had forgotten about being wild. In fact, they remembered how good water tasted. Of course, like a lot of wild things, they stayed wild. But tying a foreleg to the back leg with a side line will change the mind of wild ones running off. It will at least slow them down. But sometimes drovers ran out of rope. Then they would fit toothpicks between the eyelids to hold them open. When a critter couldn't blink its eyes, it couldn't see well. Thus, the cattle would be more manageable and move along where the drovers wanted them to go.

One morning before breakfast, after gathering about fifty heads using the methods described above, a visitor, a Swede, walked into camp. All along the trail, these brush poppers had adorned the dialect of plenty, like Indians, Mexicans, and Texans—but seldom a Swede.

"Shee twist herr heed offe," said the Swede, who was maybe six feet up and about two hundred fifty down. This fellow was all fellow.

Boss Marting and Bill Gauge tried mind reading. Maybe the "herr" was a woman who had fallen down a tree, got her "heed" caught in a fork, and "twist herr heed offe." That was about all these two could figure.

The drovers were amazed at the talk and gestures of the Swede's head and hands. That was about the only way this fellow could communicate to them. Then one of the drovers remembered Swede talk like that, and he also knew of a mine being worked east of there. The three drovers concluded this fellow was most likely a w——k Swede. Anyway, he seemed to be in hot water up to his knees, so the drovers saddled up and followed him down a brushy canyon, up a brushy draw, then out onto a brushy hill. All three of them spotted a cow trail leading out into a distant valley. The fresh tracks of a cow and a footbacker were in plain sight. The story they figured was this: the big Swede was driving a cow someplace, and they had arrived at this place, but evidently, this wasn't the place where the Swede had wanted the cow to go. From the looks of the signs on the trail, the cow didn't want to go the way the Swede wanted to go and tried dodging around him and his horse; the Swede, though, turned her back. In fact, the Swede did such a good job that the cow went down an embankment—and there she lay at the bottom with "herr heed twist offe!" The cow had slipped down the incline and caught her head under a six-inch exposed pipe. The momentum flipped the cow over the pipe, and she came to rest on the other side.

All three drovers agreed with the big Swede that she had "twist herr heed offe." So they got their ketch ropes and hooked them on to the cow, and the four used all their might to pull that old bossy back into circulation. And the big Swede was glad to know his cow hadn't "twist herr heed off."

On that same trip, the drovers picked up some more Chain C cattle, but at a cost. One big yearling got his neck broke. They figured that on the account of the cow. In addition, three heads were crippled. But the men gathered another forty or so heads of grown stock. These too would be put in the water trap. The next day they would go back for the crippled and pack in for beef the yearling with the broken neck. Like I said, they had good luck and bad luck.

III

The cow hunters had been gone two months now. The drover and Boss Martin closed the final gate on forty heads. Charley stayed behind bringing in the crippled. Now the rough count was up to around eight hundred heads. That was about what the guess had been when they started. What was paid at the beginning was way under that count. Not bad for two months' work. The drover told Mr. Ward that a cow buyer would visit him on a certain day, and on that day, he would turn the final herd over to him. So it went. Not until the drover saw the six-figure numbers in his bank account did he believe it, and not until he saw the bank president, Monroe, did he realize the bank wished him all the worst kind of bad luck and would go out their way to cause it.

By late summer, the drover got word from a thrashing crew that was working a field in the Chain C country that there were thirty heads and a big old bull grazing on the stubble field. So the group saddled up and headed south again. This time, Bill Gauge took a big wagon with them.

They had a delightful surprise that night when camp was pitched. When Bill unloaded the bedrolls, a big Rhode Island hen flew out from under the wagon box. Seems that the box had been her home all summer. Well, when they fed the horses, they fed the chicken too. When they bedded down for the night, she roosted on a wagon wheel. And then there was an egg laid under the wagon box. So the men had eggs for breakfast. It just took two weeks this time!

Forty more heads were gathered along with a fine young range bull. This time the drover knew what he would do. A brand was recorded, and that brand, fleur-de-lis, was stamped on the left side of all the stock, which was turned loose in pastures closer to home.

IV

It wasn't all cow gathering in those days either, as so many roundup stories—provided, mind you, by the best storytellers—would have you believe. Word got to the drover there was to be a celebration at Seymour. So the wife and kids were gathered up, the team was harnessed, and the buggy was packed. The whole family would go on this one hundred-mile trip. The celebration was going to be more like a reunion. The wife noticed the old familiar faces of those who had driven herds long ago on the trail north. Why was Elie there, he had come in all the way from Fort Worth. Why, he was one the drover had sold stock to down at the stockyards. There was Sands from way down

South Texas way, and Kenyon, who had come in from the Plains county. Yep, it would be trail-herding time without any herd. The reunion would be filled with old trail drivers who gathered in bunches repeating, "The last time we went up this trail..." But you never heard one remark about one coming back down the trail!

The railroad had also just laid tracks into town, bringing more to this powwow. Some of the Kiowa tribe also attended, for they know cow drovers had hiccup water somewhere. Then there was a big, live train steam engine setting there with steam hissing out. Some of the old drovers were eyeing that fellow setting in the cab. They hadn't forgotten horses just don't cotton to steam whistles. And those old drovers were probably wondering if this fellow might get all overjoyed and use some of that steam. Or perhaps that fellow had been on one of those trains that had to shut out the lights going through one of those cow towns. Maybe he'd just be satisfied with fresh-cooked buffalo chunks and potato salad. Then there was the big old black smoke funnel up there on the boiler. As the men were sizing up the trainmen, a big old Kiowa Indian roped that funnel off the steam boiler. That drew a little attention from the railroad men. Some crewmen picked it up and set it back in place, and the celebration went on. Some rancher had saved a few heads of buffalo and had a special place for them on this ranch. But two big yearlings went into the cook pit.

The drover ran across his old Emiline, a companion of the trail dust. Emiline was a good hand with horses. That made him a wild bronc rider. Emiline would take chances with his life trying to save others in danger.

Part of this celebration consisted of local talent, that is, a little show that would exhibit the trying times of just what might have taken place on the trails of long ago. This little show took place on open ground, not in a show ring. But it was not a show-off show. In those days, it was fun and friendship for all—even the horses. That evening, Emiline busted three broncs to a standstill. The show was judged by how many broncs a fellow could ride, not by somebody blowing on a horn. These were drovers, not those so-called "cowboys of the stopwatch." Let me tell you a little about Emiline. He was a master bronc rider. He could put a silver dollar in each stirrup, under his boots, and those coins would still be there when the bronc quit bucking.

After the bronc-riding contest, a big steer, about thirteen hands high, was gathered. He was then turned loose, and he went plowing off toward the distant trees and, of course, the brush. Emiline had a line back dun horse. And he was fast. The horse overtook the steer in a few strides, and in a short time the big steer lay on the ground. Emiline proved his command of the steer by tailing it. Some fellows call this Californian, just because the Spaniards used this method. But around these parts, tailing means riding alongside the rumbling critter, catching the long tail, and dangling the bushy part around the saddle horn. One step to the side and Mr. Steer would sure have changed his mind about quitting the herd. There is a trick to this method, and if not done correctly, a couple of fingers can be separated from a good hand. Then if necessary, the drover jumps off the horse and ties the steer's hind legs together before he gets up. The drover had wished he could have done such a job on those steers back in the Indian nation. That was before the buckskins had run him all the way back to the cow wagon!

That night, the fiddlers cranked up in a big old church house, the only big building in town. The furniture was lined up around the walls, and the music makers gathered in the pulpit. The drover and his missus could not help but notice, as the night moved on, that certain man was getting sweet on a certain woman. Along about daylight, the celebration dance began winding down, and the drover and company headed for the pallets to pick up the sleeping kids. This certain couple, who had danced all night, were then joined by another man. He said seven words: "Get the kids, and let's go home."

But morning was still not-going-home time. Coffee was made by the gallons. The buffalo was heated up while pans of biscuits started rising in the ovens along with some tasty sweets. It might be years before all these old hands would see one another again.

After a little rest, another contest began. This was nothing like bronco busting, roping, or steer tailing. This would be goose pulling. In those days, food was a serious commodity. One chance would be all the chance one had to fetch it—the fetcher had better be good—either with a gun, knife, or slingshot. Contests like turkey shooting from remarkable distances would test the player's skill at providing. But today a wagonload of geese was brought in for a goose-pulling contest. A goose was hung up by its legs about as high as a head on a horse, usually in a nearby tree the same way a thief who steals horses is punished. A good coat of grease was then applied around the head and neck. The idea was to race by horseback, then take the goose's head off by catching it with one hand—a real wobbly feat. It's fast business and not so easy to do. The drover won. He figured out a way of turning his hand over and avoiding the grease. They took twenty heads of geese home! Some went in the pot, and some went to the stock watering hole, a tank. But the missus wasn't too pleased with her husband's starched white shirt for it was covered with blood. I'll tell you why she had a right to be angry, for she, like the other women of her time, had to do her wash in a cast-iron pot that set on an open fire. Starching was done the same way. The ironing was done with an iron that set on a cookstove until it got hot. (And don't forget, some poor soul had to cut wood for all this business.) That was in those days.

V

On one trip up north, the drover, Bill Gauge, and Boss Martin rounded up and cow hunted the Block brand cattle. This company offered the same kind of deal the Chain C Company had offered. The land the men would have to work in this time had similar conditions as their last roundup with the Chain C Company, only there was not so much brush, but the deep canyons made up for that. Using the same techniques, the drover caught about eleven hundred heads of wild cattle. They drove them into town and locked them in the railroad pens. Then the pendulum of luck started to swing the other way. The drovers couldn't get stock cars from the railroad. They also had to get hay feed and fill the water troughs. Shipping cattle out of here was going to be a problem, but in a few days it would start making a big difference, especially on the pocketbooks.

Down at the hotel—the only one in town—the drover just happened to run across another cowman. It was not quite by accident. The three had been waiting around the hotel to hear something from the railroad. After feeding and watering the stock, one of the men started playing dominoes. There was another stockman who was also waiting on stock cars. This stranger seemed to favor the drover. After all, the drover was more interested in shipping his cattle than playing dominoes. The stranger then took him aside and told him there was a big ranch up north a ways that owned a train. In fact, they were going to ship cattle to Fort Worth. They could make a deal with them—and they did. When the last cow was loaded and the cattle car bolted, the drover returned to the hotel to pick up his gear. The domino player was still playing dominoes! As the drover was fixing to leave town, the stranger waved good-bye. The drover was moving out, he wasn't moving dominoes. His attitude was, "I'm moving and not settin'. As long as there is settin', there won't be no movin'." Well, maybe that there fellow just liked the game.

THE BUG AND CANDLE POWER

On one particular trip out to West Texas, the drover, Boss Martin, and Bill Gauge were helping someone else move a herd of cattle. There was a particular fellow who had recently joined the crew. A judgment could not be passed on looks—actions maybe. Well, this fellow looked like a bug, acted like one, and more or less thought like one. You know, a bug crawls and walks around in a wishy-washy way, then it starts becoming a cocklebur under a saddle blanket, and something like a cocklebur seems to magnify itself and press a point, especially on someone else.

The men came up with a plan. No big swatting, though. First, they found a large dipper gourd. A dipper gourd has a long neck and an end like a round ball. A person can make a drinking vessel by splitting this critter down the middle. But this one was going to stay whole. One the big end of the gourd, one of the men cut a slot. On the handle end, they fastened a long cord. This cord would not be pulled over a tree limb so one of them could set behind a bush and operate it. Then a lighted candle would be placed in the hollowed-out place where the slot was. Of course, this operation was going to take place at nighttime. They knew Bug rode over to the river store on Sunday night.

Their plan was falling into place. The gourd was rigged with a lighted candle and tested hanging out over the road. Behind good, thick brush, the man who had control of the cord could pull back on it and up would go a light. If the operator gave it slack, down it would go along the ground. Oh yeah, this was going to work like a charm! All the three needed to do now was wait for the sound of Bug's return, light the candle, and create all kinds of sounds. At the given time, the lighted gourd would be pulled up high in a brushy limb. Bug wouldn't notice it as he trotted close by. Just before he and his horse went under it, the men would have to hold back much laughter.

The night was plenty dark, with only twinkling stars above. The horse and rider were getting in range. Bug was about five yards off when the lighted gourd began to make its slow descent. It hovered above the ground then made its slow rise back up into the tree.

Both the horse and the rider spotted this thing coming down. It wasn't necessary for too much of a show, especially for the horse. He done made up his mind for Bug. That horse just wasn't going to go down that road! Those horses' eyes became part of the twinkling stars, and his screaming whinny could be heard clear back at the river! The rider, agreeing with the horse, twisted off the road and tore through some thick brush which wasn't to the rider's liking.

The three men kept hearing the brush breaking down, but they were so busy laughing that they didn't notice the lighted gourd still going up and down. When they did, they thought they were witnessing a real supernatural phenomenon because they knew nobody was now working that long cord. The whole contraption then took off and bounced through dark tree limbs; the lighted candle was flickering like curly hairs in a breeze. A rush of wind helped the gourd go even higher. Then it seemed to come to a halt in mid sky.

The pranksters didn't know the end of the cord had gotten caught on a bush. When the wind settled, the gourd hit the ground, and the candle went out. That was about the same time the ghost makers decided to tear down some more brush for themselves! After a heated run back to the cow wagon, the men hunkered down in their bedrolls. The idea of Bug coming back and pulling a funny on them kind of entered their minds. But they knew Bug wouldn't be back so soon, for his horse was still running.

The next morning, the three decided to have another look at that terrible place. The gourd was still on the ground, but the cord was gone. Then they saw this big old owl building its nest close to the same tree the gourd had been hooked to. For the want of a shoe a horse was lost, for the want of a string a nest was built.

THE TANGLED KETCH ROPE

A ranch in south Texas needed a man to gather some cattle. They did not mention these things were wild as a windstorm. I was the man they were looking for. Now I ain't no greenhorn. I learned the trade at a very tender age. I started breaking and training horses at the age of thirteen. This followed a thought to Fort Sill, Oklahoma. This was where a bronc was rode till he quit bucking. Then the shoulder boy took him over and the officer-in-charge presented a one-dollar bill. Of course as many as eight heads could be snapped out in one day. That is "effen" your head didn't get busted. Maybe more. In those days, that was quite a bankroll.

A feller at Fort Summers, New Mexico, needed a bronc twister, so I went. The folks that do not know what Fort Summers sets on, there are plenty of rolling land. The fact is there's so much there, there's not enough for the sun to set on.

Fact is a bronc could run away with you—cold-jaws on you; it means letting him run until his mainspring runs down. Then he might start paying attention of what was expected of doing a job. The Matador Ranch in West Texas, a place for ranch horses to have wall-eyed fits, was waiting for the so-called rider to fit his saddle on him.

The Matador Ranch is a place in West Texas where some of the onerous, so-called saddle horse ever drew a breath of air. Some of our older hands called them other kinds of names. I often wondered why some of these ranch horses were not put in the rodeo circuit. There was a claybank pony that carried his "off ear" laid down. This was a sign for the feller setting in the saddle: "I don't like you worth a flip." This particular cowboy waited until he got to a rock pile; there is where the flip became reality. I didn't mind this so much as the dag-gum horse nickering about his success. Of these same kinds of horses, a thousand-pound steer could be roped and tied to a gentle tree. The worst cow-gathering I remember was in a place that was called Crotten Breaks. Crotten Oil. For those who don't know what that little tidbit is; this place got its name honorable. This was part of the Matador Ranch Co. This is still a rough part of creation. I say now some of them bovines just didn't want to come out of their homeland. They were roped and pulled up to the flat land. There have been many a saddle horses; also, the one that sat atop him that has been crippled in the Garden of Eden.

So after twenty-five years, I thought I was a professional. That was right, but unseen things seemed to take a different point of view. I reckon the hidden meaning is this: the word would be fate. I believe that is a procured state of mind. Any rider that is protected to gather wild cattle soon becomes the same learning thing. "Effen" they stay with it long enough," but a life is a life wherever it may be.

I set out to the ranch in south Texas. A big river ran right through the hundred and ten thousand acres of brush, brush, and brush. I did not take my own horses, which one day I regretted. I used the ranch horses to gather these so-called cattle that no brush popper could gather. That was because they didn't want to.

A Mexican ranch hand and I were "prowling" the river one hot day in June. There's an old ranch saying "They got to come water some time." These profuse words were soon fulfilled. The Mexican and I slid our horses down the riverbank to where the water skipped along the bed. The bed was the river bottom. Cow trails meandered here and there. They came to water here. Water took up about half this riverbed. There were shallows and deep holes. In flow times, the water washed out deeper holes, especially in the bends of the river. But at this time of year, the water was down to a trickle. But theses deep holds were kept full of water. Here is where the bovines watered.

Ridden around a brushy bend, there he was. I said he because I can tell a girl from a boy. About six hundred pounds of stuff. I motioned for the Mexican to climb out and keep him from going on down the riverbed. I would stay here and be quiet as a church mouse. Once this critter figured something was up, he was off to the wild blue yonder. Carlos slid his horse off the riverbank in front of that yearling. Of course this wild one spotted a man on a horse. He turned tail toward me. When he came around the river bend, I had my rope with a loop in the end of it ready.

There was no running, I just pulled alongside, and this critter stuck his head in this ready-made loop. I turned this bay horse to take up the slack in the rope. I can't remember what the ranch hands called him, or named him, but what was fixing to take place I added a few more words. He took up the slack all right and took the bridle bite in mouth also. I had no control over the yearling much less this crazy goofy thing my saddle was cinched to.

The only thing I remember was bucking, bawling, and having wild-eyed fits. This wild yearling's broadside wasn't helping a bit. Much less what matters. Instead of heading for the deep sand of the riverbed, this goofy bay horse headed for one of these deep holes of water. A freight train couldn't turn him.

During all this grunting and groaning, a slack did from in this ketch rope. In fact, it formed a half hitch on my right leg. This is what they call the offside. When this outfit hit the deep water, I and this goofy bay horse went under. This yearling managed to keep a taut rope around my leg. Goofy bay hit the bottom and come up. Of course, so did I. The wild thing that was on the end of this ketch rope and this goofy horse of which I had no control. The yearling jerked me out of the saddle.

That dang half hitch had me by my leg. This time I was behind goofy. I could feel those hind feet missing me by inches. He was still trying to pitch and have wall-eyed fits in deep water. I went down again. By this time, it didn't seem to make much difference. I was going to drown. Seems I did not mind. Weakness was taking over in such a short time. It seemed like hours being hooked onto a crazy, goofy horse and a wild yearling for company in deep water.

I don't know what happened. I believe the dark veil was erased by some word of reasoning. That crazy bay came up again, and I felt that half hitch come off my leg. I came free. But I still had a way to go. By this time, Carlos came wading in the shallow water to pull me out of the deep. With boots full of water, a pair of bull-hide leggings on, a leather brush jumper—a feller can't float too good in water. Carlos dragged me up on dry land. I looked down, and I still had the bridal reins in my hand. That goofy horse was still going crazy. Carlos pulled me up on dry, dry land. There by the stroke of faith. I lay there a good long time.

There was this bay horse still rolling around in the water. Carlos got the bridle reigns and pulled his head up out of the water. When something like this takes place, there is nothing anyone can do to stop it. Only stand by and watch what the outcome will be. Using the water, we pulled him on the water's edge. This goofy thing we call a horse had inhaled about two hundred gallons of water. He was breathing pretty hard, and so was I.

Carlos and I pulled him closer to the water's edge. Old goofy was lying broadside. Carlos pulled his nose up out of the water. I've seen fellers get drowned in the South Pacific during WWII, and they went through the same spasms. His nose was on dry land, but that water-logged goofy bay horse lying broadside looked like he had supped up half the water in that hole.

I don't know how long I lay around that "wishing well," but there were two cigarette butts where Carlos squatted. Finally, old water dog, goofy, crazy bay came back to life. With a liquid heave and a few gurgles, he stood up on all fours. My saddle was setting atop a great big water barrel. A camel could not have taken on that much water. By now, goofy, crazy bay was as peaceful as a baby with a milk bottle.

I took hold of the bridle reigns and led him up on dry land. This bay horse belched up about five gallons of water. I was not in kind of indifference. Carlos came leading his horse and rolling a currley. "Commea," I said, "La Vaca." Carlos just lowered his shoulders and started rolling another currley. Where that yearling went, I never knew. My ketch rope was tied hard and fast to the saddle horn. Some things hover down on a person. Some think one thing, and some

CPSIA information can be obtained
at www.ICGtesting.com
Printed in the USA
LVOW04s2053120816
500060LV00016B/159/P